James R. R, Renell, Consort of Frederick III, Empress Victoria

Frederick Crown Prince and Emperor

James R. R, Renell, Consort of Frederick III, Empress Victoria

Frederick Crown Prince and Emperor

ISBN/EAN: 9783337270902

Printed in Europe, USA, Canada, Australia, Japan

Cover: Foto ©Andreas Hilbeck / pixelio.de

More available books at **www.hansebooks.com**

FREDERICK

CROWN PRINCE AND EMPEROR

From a Photograph by Messrs. Reichard & Lindner, of Berlin.

FREDERICK

CROWN PRINCE AND EMPEROR

A Biographical Sketch Dedicated to His Memory

BY

RENNELL RODD

WITH AN INTRODUCTION BY

HER MAJESTY THE EMPRESS FREDERICK

" He was as full of kindness as of valour,
Princely in both"

NEW YORK
MACMILLAN AND CO.
1888

CONTENTS.

INTRODUCTION—   PAGE

Letter from Her Majesty the Empress Frederick vii

Preface xiii

CHAPTER   I. 1831—1848........................ 17

   ,,   II. 1848—1858................................ 35

   ,,   III. 1858—1863.. 59

   ,,   IV. 1864—1869............................... 75

   ,,   V. 1870—1871............ 99

   ,,   VI. 1871—1887 143

   ,,   VII. 1888.................................... 175

APPENDIX 189

Dear Mr. Rodd,

I think you are aware
that my beloved husband, the late Emperor
Frederick, when in England last year, visited
the Throat Hospital, and was full of com-
passion for the patients. His ailment caused
at that time but little inconvenience, and
his kind heart felt deeply sorry for those
who had more to bear from the state of
their throats. I had then a great wish to
help the Hospital in some way, and had
intended to make some little drawings, and
collect some pretty and amusing stories to

form a small book which could be sold for
the benefit of the Hospital funds. Alas! I
never found leisure or peace of mind to
carry out this plan.

As I have witnessed how much can be
done by medical skill and careful nursing
to alleviate the condition of those who suffer,
I feel doubly anxious that as many as
possible of those who have to struggle with
sickness should be able to gain admission
to a Hospital where they can find care and
comforts which they could not have at home,
and the best chance of being cured. Now
that I have seen the kind and sincere
sympathy with which my own countrymen
followed the course of my beloved husband's
illness, and the true feeling they showed in
mourning his loss, I feel emboldened to take
up under another form my idea of helping
the Hospital. Not my own drawings or
writings would I offer, but I ask you to
pen a short account of the life of my beloved

husband, who was so soon taken away from us. As you knew him in sunny days when he was the picture of life and health, as well as in the last sad year when that life was overshadowed by sickness, I thought none would be better able than you to undertake the task of writing a short biography suitable for popular reading, which may make his name better known to the English Public, and give him a place in their affections beside that of my father, for whom he had so great a love, admiration and veneration, and with whose views and aims he so truly sympathized. I feel sure that the life of a good and noble man must be interesting to all, and that an example so bright and pure can only do good.

Those in humbler walks of life who are denied many of the blessings enjoyed by the rich, to whose lot fall the so-called good things of this world, are often apt to imagine that their burden is the hardest to bear, that

struggles, and pain, and tears are only for
them.   These perhaps will think differently
when they read of sufferings borne with such
patience, and of duty so cheerfully performed
while sickness was undermining the strength
of the strong man ; they will be able to enter
in some degree into the depths of regret and
disappointment felt by a ruler who loved his
people, at being unable to carry out the long
cherished plans for the welfare that he had so
much at heart ; they will gaze with admiration
at the courage with which, when the shades of
death were hanging over his path, he strode
stedfastly along to the end.

Grief and pain come alike to all ; broken
hearts are to be found in palaces as well as in
cottages, and the bond of brotherhood seems
strongest when love and pity unite all hearts,
and reverence for what is good lifts up our
souls.   May this little history of the good and
useful life of the Emperor Frederick appeal to
the hearts of those who read it, and be as it

were a greeting from him to his fellow sufferers
in the Hospital, to whom I so earnestly desire
to do a small service ; and to which you have
so kindly promised to devote your pen.

Yrs sincerly

Victoria

PREFACE.

THE following brief sketch contains nothing controversial, nothing which could lead to dispute or discussion, and it has been especially attempted to eliminate, as far as possible, all matter of a political nature, and confine it to the record of such facts as illustrate the character of a simple and noble life, in a manner which may be acceptable to that wider circle of readers for whom, in accordance with the desire expressed in the introduction, it is designed. It is incomplete, inasmuch as it contains the story of one life, which is so intimately bound up with another, that the picture could only be completed by a full account of the lives of both. But it is believed that the intention of one, in obedience to whose wishes it was undertaken, has been thus best fulfilled.

R. R.

October, 1888.

I.

1831—1848.

I.

1831—1848.

THE Emperor Frederick was born on the 18th
of October, 1831, the anniversary of the battle
of Leipzig, and on the 18th of June, 1888, the
anniversary of the battle of Waterloo, he was
carried to his last resting-place in the church
dedicated to Peace, among the gardens of Sans
Souci.   It is a curious coincidence that a life
which will be for ever associated in history
with the union of the German race into the
great Empire of to-day should have opened
and closed upon the anniversaries of these two
great victories.   In the fierce light of modern
days, when nothing remains secret or sacred,
where every action is watched by a thousand
jealous eyes, interpreted or misinterpreted by a
thousand busy voices, we do not always
recognize our heroes when they come : but

B

the immediate verdict of contemporaries found him worthy of the time he was born in, and of the great events he was called upon to assist in moulding. Placed in that lofty station which at least escapes the eye of scrutiny, he was found true to his own princely ideal as son, as husband, as father ; true to the ideal of his countrymen as a fearless leader in the battlefield, true to the highest ideal of all times as man and prince ; and surely, wherever the story is told of the great decade which closed with the proclamation of the German Empire at Versailles, beside the three figures which dominate it, the darling hero of future generations of Germans will be the Prince who taught the North and South their common brotherhood, whom Saxons, Bavarians, Würt-tembergers, and Badenese, no less than Prussians, alike saluted by the name of " Unser Fritz."

Those who have witnessed the events of the last months, have all been touched according to the depth of their own natures by the brave endurance and resignation, by the deeply pathetic close of a life, which, with its great opportunities for good and evil, was spent in

unceasing devotion to duty, in patient prepara-
tion for yet greater responsibilities, in unwearying efforts for the good of others.   And yet
probably what will remain to after generations,
when the passions and emotions of life around
them engage all their attention, and the keen
interest with which we have followed the events
of the past year is absorbed in other lives, will
be that radiant and heroic figure, which
children's eyes will follow on the canvases
depicting the triumph of Germany, of the
soldier-prince, who, in the hour of danger and
uncertainty, succeeded in uniting the sympathies of North and South, and guided that
irresistible wave of national feeling through
the bloody fields of Weissenburg and Wörth,
by the great strategic march to the crowning
victory of Sedan.   It may not be the immor-
tality he would himself have chosen, but no
man is master of his fate, and where so much
must needs be left undone, where so many
hopes and aspirations were disappointed, this
at least will remain for ever associated with
the most imperishable traditions of a great
nation, of a Prince who did all things well.
History has but few such figures to show us,

B 2

and the record of their lives is soon told.
The evil genius of many of the great characters
of story has filled innumerable volumes, but a
few lines will keep green the memory of our
Sydneys and our Bayards.   As with nations,
we say they are happiest who afford least
material to the historian ; so perhaps with
great men, in proportion to the nobility and
simplicity of their lives the work of the bio-
grapher becomes easier, and truly of the
Emperor Frederick, we may say as of few
others who have lived so much before the
world :

> " He kept
> " The whitness of his soul, and thus men o'er
>   him wept."

In the year that ushered in the birth of the
young Prince, the most sanguine of patriots
would scarcely have ventured to prophecy the
imminent ascendency of the Prussian star.
King Frederick William III., who had already
occupied the throne for thirty-four years, had
seen the disastrous days of Jena and Auerstadt,
and had devoted himself to the great task of
the restoration of his country.   He had shared
in the victories which ended in the overthrow

of Napoleon, and after the long and troublous reign, which he epitomized himself in one proverbial sentence, "My days in unrest, but my hope in God," desired only to end his life in peace.

The dream of German unity had made but little progress. It was the interest of Austria and Russia to see that their Prussian neighbour should find no means of expansion, and the conservatism of the smaller German states looked with no friendly eye on a capital where the spirit of opposition to the old order was most rife, and the speeches and writings of the new school of politicians assumed a more violent character.

The Crown Prince had married some eight years previously Princess Elizabeth of Bavaria, and the marriage had remained childless. His younger brother Prince William was therefore the heir presumptive, and it was the occasion for no ordinary rejoicing when his marriage with Princess Augusta of Saxe Weimar was blessed two years later with the birth of a son, and a direct hereditary succession was thus guaranteed in the house of Hohenzollern.

The Prince was born in the palace to which

as Emperor he gave the name of Friedrichskron,
known till then only as the New Palace of Sans
Souci, the largest and the finest of the many
palaces of Potsdam, to which his parents had
then retired on account of the cholera, which
was raging at that time in Berlin.   It was built
by Frederick the Great immediately after the
close of the Seven Years' War, to the confusion
of those who thought that his treasury was
exhausted, but which had hitherto been little
used.   It was this palace that in later years, as
Crown Prince, the Emperor Frederick made his
summer residence ; here most of his children
were born, here all the interests and pursuits of
country life were fostered and enjoyed, here
were the brightest associations of a happy
home, and it was hither that he came to die.
The Mark of Brandenburg is for the most part
a flat unlovely district of sandy plains alternat-
ing with wide tracts of fir forest, but, in the
neighbourhood of Potsdam, the river Havel,
widening in a series of considerable lakes surrounded with undulating wooded shores, has
formed a pleasant oasis, and there are few
prettier spots in the early summer months than
the gardens and Park of Sans Souci, at the

further end of which, about a mile and a half from Potsdam, stands the great Rococo Palace of Friedrichskron.

The christening took place on the 13th of November, in the presence of the King, the Crown Prince, and all the members of the Royal Family. The absent god-parents, the Empresses of Austria and Russia, were represented by their respective Ambassadors, and the baby Prince received from Bishop Eylert the names of Frederick William Nicholas Charles.

The Princes of the House of Hohenzollern become soldiers almost from the cradle. Prince William, who had, while still a mere boy, entered Paris with the Allies, took a keen delight in the military education of his son, and the little Prince was only eight years old when, together with two young playfellows,* he was put through his drill in a miniature private's uniform, and acquitted himself as a most capable recruit, under the orders of his instructor, Sergeant Bludau. Of the qualities which he inherited from his parents it is not necessary to speak. The courage, simplicity, integrity, and

* Rudolf v. Zastrow and Count Adolf Königsmark.

kindliness of the aged Emperor, who was in a
truer sense than any who have borne the title
the " father of his people," are known to all the
present generation. But of the friends and
playfellows of his youth many have now passed
away, and it may be interesting here to record
that there was no one to whom, in these early
days, he was more fondly attached than Princess
Charlotte of Prussia, who afterwards became
Hereditary Princess of Meiningen, and mother
of his future son-in-law. He was also much
with his cousins Prince Frederick Charles and
the two sisters of the latter. Princess, afterwards Queen Elizabeth, the wife of King
Frederick William IV., had no children of her
own, but it was her especial pleasure to gather
her young nephews and nieces round her, and
be a second mother to them.

Prince Frederick William never forgot her
kindness to him as a child ; and when she died
at Dresden, in 1873, after twelve years of
widowhood, he took upon himself the duties of
a son, and performed the last offices of kindness,
bringing home her body to lay it beside her
husband in the Church of Peace, at Sans Souci.
The friendship formed in childhood for his

cousin, Prince Frederick Charles, continued into later life, when their mimic games of war, with their respective corps of cadets, became the grim earnest of the battlefield. They were appointed Field-Marshals upon the same day, when the news of the fall of Metz reached the headquarters of the German Army at Versailles; and by a singular coincidence their deaths took place on the same day of the month, and at the same hour of the day, at the same interval of three years that had separated their births.

The education of Prince Frederick William began under the auspices of Frau von Clausewitz, widow of the well-known General, and Madame Godet, his governess, a Swiss lady from Neufchatel, whose son became, a few years later, the Prince's first tutor. In 1844, when he had reached his thirteenth year, the noted German Hellenist, Dr. Ernest Curtius, was chosen to superintend his studies. No branch of general culture was neglected; music and dancing, gymnastics and fencing, were all taught betimes, and the handicraft of bookbinding was selected for the young Prince to master, in accordance with the family

tradition that all the Princes of the Royal
House shall acquire practical knowledge of
some trade.

In the meantime several events occurred to
break the quiet routine of study. In 1838 a
sister was born, and christened Louise, after
her grandmother, the Queen, whose beauty,
courage and misfortunes, have made her the
heroine of Prussian patriotism. In 1840 King
Frederick William III. died, and the little
Prince was, for the first time, brought face to
face with death. In accordance with precedent,
Prince William now assumed the title of Prince
of Prussia, and he was appointed by his brother,
who had ascended the throne under the name
of Frederick William IV., Stadtholder of Pomerania. On reaching his tenth year, Prince
Frederick William received a commission as
Second Lieutenant in the First Regiment of the
Infantry of the Guard. He was presented to
the officers of the regiment by his uncle, the
King, who said to him : " You are but a little
fellow as yet, Fritz, but do your best to get to
know these gentlemen, and some day you will
be their overseer, however much they may now
see over you.'

A military instructor was now attached to the Prince in the person of Colonel, afterwards General von Unruh, in company with whom, or with his tutor, Dr. Curtius, he began to make short journeys in the neighbouring provinces and states. Thus he visited the towns and islands of the Baltic, and made walking tours through the Harz, Thuringia, Saxon Switzerland, and the Giant Mountains, acquiring that taste for travel which he preserved in later years, and studying by personal observation " the cities and customs of many men." Otherwise, his summers were spent at Babelsberg, in the neighbourhood of Potsdam, the country seat which the Prince of Prussia had himself planned and executed, and which became his favourite country residence as King and Emperor.

It was here that the young Prince remained in seclusion with his mother through the troubled days of 1848, when the February Revolution at Paris gave the signal for outbreaks in other continental cities. The concessions which the Liberal party had anticipated from the reigning Sovereign had not been granted, and the insurrectionists were for a

time masters of the situation in Berlin. A
spirit of self-sacrifice induced the Prince of
Prussia to take upon himself a large portion
of the popular resentment, and the future hero
of German unity lightened his brother's task
in re-establishing order, by withdrawing for
a while from Berlin, and appearing to remove in his person the menace of the military
element, against which a great part of the
general discontent was directed. His intrepid
character, however, resented giving colour
to the appearance of flight, and he only
left on receiving written orders from the
King to proceed immediately upon a special
mission to London, and report to the Court
of St. James on recent developments at
Berlin.

Prince Frederick William was then just at
that age when, on the threshold of manhood,
the mind is most impressionable, and, unbiased
by the teachings of past experience, is apt to
review with an immediate judgment the merits
of current events. The scenes which he had
lately witnessed could not fail to have a deep
and lasting effect upon his generous and
reflective character. The Throne recovered its

ascendancy, but only after large concessions and a reform of the Constitution ; the national voice had found expression, and a new phase of national development opened for the new generation. Early in June the Prince of Prussia returned, and signified his adhesion to the remodelled Constitution ; the Princess, with her children, travelled as far as Magdeburg to greet him on his return, and the rest of the summer was spent at Babelsberg, where the young Prince was prepared for his Confirmation, which took place in the chapel at Charlottenburg on September 29th. In the Spring of the following year, he was present at the solemn audience at which King Frederick William IV. refused the Imperial Crown of Germany, which the Frankfort Parliament proposed to confer upon him, little anticipating how fully, some twenty years later, the words which fell from his uncle's lips were destined to be realized : "*An Imperial Crown must be won upon the field of battle.*"

The Prince was now in his eighteenth year, the age at which the Royal Princes enter upon active service in the army. His military education had been completed under General von Unruh, and, afterwards, under Major von Natzmer and Colonel Fischer — and so the chapter of boyhood closes. It cannot close better than with a quotation from a letter which the Princess of Prussia wrote to the playfellow and comrade of her son, Rudolf von Zastrow, who was also entering the world, and about to pass his examinations for the army, for it illustrates the nature of the home-influences under which their youth had passed.

"Life is full of difficulties and seductions of every kind, we must therefore daily pray for strength to combat them, that we may remain true to our principles. The superficialities of life often neutralize our taste for serious occupation; we must remember that we have something to learn every day, and that we shall not retain what we have learnt, if we fail to make our knowledge complete. What is most of all to be desired is the harmonious union of character and heart. Happy are they to whom God grants these qualities. I believe that you possess them. My prayer is that you may always be a son to me, and that separation may not weaken this tie. In me you will always find a friend, a mother. And next I pray you always to remain a friend, a brother, to my son. Princes seldom have real friends. His heart requires a friendship of this kind, and you may serve him in a number of ways. You have promised me this, and I rely upon your gratitude as well as your word of honour." *

* This letter is given in full in "L'Empereur Frédéric," by Edouard Simon, from which this extract is translated.

II.

1848—1858.

C

II.

On the 3rd of May, 1849, Prince Frederick
William entered upon active service with the
regiment to which he was attached. The
Prince of Prussia introduced him to the
assembled officers with a few spirited words,
in which he spoke feelingly of the admirable
discipline shown by the army in the recent
troubles, and of the sympathy and fidelity
which his old comrades had testified towards
himself. " I entrust my son to you," he said,
" in the hope that he will learn obedience, and
so some day know how to command ; " and to
his son he simply said, " Now go and do your
duty!" A month later the Prince was
advanced to the rank of First Lieutenant. The
Prince of Prussia was at this period appointed
to command the army sent to put down the

c 2

military insurrection in Baden. He was
accompanied on this expedition by the young
Prince Frederick Charles, who was three years
senior to his cousin. Twenty years later the
two Princes received the Field-Marshal's bâton
upon the same day ; and now the elder Prince
was to see soldiering in earnest for the first
time. But it was judged prudent not to send
the future heir to the Prussian throne upon the
ungrateful mission of repressing an internal
revolt.

In October, upon completing his eighteenth
year, Prince Frederick William came of age,
according to precedent in the royal family of
Prussia, and was solemnly invested with the
Order of the Black Eagle, the highest Prussian
order, which corresponds most nearly to the
Garter in England. The young Prince's first
quoted public utterance is the message in
which he thanked the Municipality of Potsdam
for their congratulations on this occasion : " I
am still very young," he said, " but I will pre-
pare myself with love and devotion for my high
calling, and endeavour some day to fulfil these
anticipations which will then become a duty
entrusted to me by God."

After a few months of service with his regiment, he left for the University of Bonn, attended by Colonel Fischer and an Aide-de-camp. It was a new departure, and typical of the changed order of ideas, that a Prince of the royal blood should enter as a student at a public university. The course of studies arranged for him formed no exception to the ordinary routine; and though he resided in the old Electoral Palace, his intercourse with the other students remained unrestricted; he attended the lectures of Dahlmann, Arndt, and Perthes, and completed his education in history, law, and literature. But his studies were not confined to the curriculum of the University. Mr. Copland Perry, who was at that time residing in Bonn, was invited to assist him in mastering the English language and literature. Mr. Perry writes: "At the Prince's request I attended on him three times a week, and had the honour of directing his studies of English history and literature, in which he took a very special interest. His love for England, and his profound admiration for our Queen, were most remarkable, and tended, of course, to render our intercourse

the more interesting and confidential. Whatever information I was able to afford him
about English political and social life was
received by him with the greatest eagerness,
and, when more solid study was concluded, we
amused ourselves by writing imaginary letters
to ministers and leaders of society."

Shortly afterwards the Prince of Prussia,
who was in 1849 appointed Military Governor
of the Rhine Provinces and Westphalia, took
up his residence at Coblenz. The reactionary
policy of the Manteuffel Cabinet did not meet
with his approval; he considered that the
pledges of 1848 must be respected, and was
glad to absent himself for a while from the
Capital, where the gatherings of the Liberal
chiefs and sympathizers at his palace were
sure to attract attention. The visits of Prince
Frederick William to Coblenz were frequent,
and led to many acquaintances and conversa-
tions on social and political topics with the
remarkable men the Princess of Prussia
gathered round her Court. During his
university career the area of his travels, which
had hitherto been confined to German territory,
was considerably extended. In 1850 he visited

Switzerland, Northern Italy, and the South of
France. The following year he accompanied
his parents to England to witness the opening
of the Great Exhibition. May-day, 1851, was
a proud day for England. The continent had
hardly recovered from the recent shocks of
revolution : France, Austria, Germany, and the
Italian States, had alike been torn by domestic
strife, but in London all the nations of the earth
had met together in friendly competition. The
scheme had not passed without considerable
opposition in England itself, but the energy and
genius of the Prince Consort, the initiator of
this international festival, had prevailed, and
set an example which other nations would not
be slow to follow. The young Prince, who also
paid a hasty visit to Liverpool and to the Isle
of Wight, carried back to Germany a deep
impression of the wealth and stability of
England, of the free spirit and reasonableness
which governed her institutions, and above all
a charming domestic picture of her happy Court,
and of a little Princess, who was then just ten
years old. He was, however, patriotic enough
to say that he preferred Babelsberg to Windsor.
Later in the year he accompanied his father on

a visit to Russia, where he was appointed
Honorary Colonel of the Eleventh Regiment of
Hussars. He rejoined his regiment at Potsdam
in time to take part in the Autumn Manœuvres,
and was advanced to the rank of Captain,
returning soon afterwards to Bonn to conclude
his university course.

At the university he first laid the foundation
of that universal popularity which characterized
the whole of his subsequent career. He
succeeded in so merging the Prince in the
student, that he was able to enter heart and
soul into the spirit of university life. He had
a word for everyone, and by those numerous
excursions in the surrounding Rhineland,
which he so particularly appreciated, he had
become a familiar figure in all the country side.
It was a source of universal regret in Bonn,
when, at Easter, 1852, the short space of time
which could be spared from the Prince's busy
life drew to its close, and town and university
vied with one another in the ovations which
marked his departure.

Returning to his regiment, the Prince devoted
himself to military duties. He was now a
Captain, and the personal interest which he took

in each individual member of his company
acquired him a proverbial popularity. During
the Autumn Manœuvres of 1853, when he was
promoted to the rank of Major, he learned the
duties of an Aide-de-camp, being attached to
the Staff of Count V. J. Groeben, who at that
time commanded the Corps of Guards. The
Prince's life was one of constant activity : under
General von Reyher he was instructed in the
special branches of the Staff; while he found
time to acquire a thorough knowledge of the
working of the various civil departments, and
devoted himself to the study of the internal
administration, under the guidance of the Chief
President of the Province of Brandenburg.
During the Summer of this year he had accompanied his father to the Manœuvres of the
Austrian Army, and was assigned by the
Emperor Franz Joseph the honorary command
of the Twentieth Regiment of Infantry. About
this period he was also initiated into the
mysteries of Freemasonry, and the Prince of
Prussia, who had taken this influential Order
under his protection, availed himself of the
occasion to protest, in his speech, against the
attempt made by a certain section in the

country, to cast discredit on this ancient
institution. In December he had an attack of
inflammation of the lungs, and after his recovery
it was considered advisable for him to spend a
Winter in the South, and thus, a long cherished
plan of a tour in Italy was carried into effect.

The royal party were conveyed from Trieste
to Ancona in an Austrian man of war, and
proceeded thence direct to Rome. The old
Papal Court was then in all its brilliancy, and
Rome was still the city of Corinne and Trans-
formation. No lines of railway pierced the
circuit of her walls, there was no gas in the
narrow alleys, but the quaint old gilded coaches
of the Cardinals, the gay uniforms of the
Papal troops, the numberless religious orders,
the costume of the people, which was then not
confined to professional models and beggars,
filled her streets with colour, and the Carnival
was still a national fête. Italian Unity had
assuredly no warmer sympathizer than Prince
Frederick William, but the Rome of his
impressions never ceased to be an interesting
and charming recollection. He was repeatedly
received with every mark of appreciation by
Pope Pius IX., who preserved a warm regard

for his royal guest, which the grave issues of
later years between Prussia and the Vatican in
no way diminished, and he assisted at the
Consistory in which the present Pontiff received
the Cardinal's Hat. The story is told that
at their first interview the Pope held out his
hand to the young Prince for the customary
kiss of homage, but the latter, as representative
of one of the two great Protestant States, did
not feel called upon to render this salute, and
warmly grasped the extended hand.   The
Pope, whose sense of humour was well known,
always at subsequent interviews greeted the
young Prince on entering with his hand behind
his back. The journey was extended to Naples
and Sicily, and the royal party returned to
Rome on their way northward to witness the
Easter ceremonies.

After six months' service with the Artillery,
Prince Frederick William was transferred to
the Dragoons of the Guard.   It may be well
here to explain that the Guards form an entire
army corps. including, therefore, infantry,
artillery. and cavalry of every arm : they
are distributed between Berlin, Potsdam, and
the neighbouring fortress of Spandau.   The

infantry regiment to which the Prince was
first attached is quartered in Potsdam; the
Dragoons of the Guard, consisting then of one
regiment only, but now of two, are stationed
in Berlin.

Colonel von Griesheim, an old friend of the
Prince of Prussia, who commanded the regiment,
has left a record of an interview which he had
with the Princess, at the time they entrusted
their son to his care.   The Princess, he says,
begged him in no way to spare his new officer,
but to let him enter into every detail of duty,
in order that he might really learn to appreciate
the hard work which military service entailed.
She bade him never lose sight of the fact that
he was to teach his future Sovereign, and that it
was essential to his forming a just appreciation of
things, that he should see their working side.
The Prince of Prussia, who came in at the close
of the interview, said, with a smile. "I taught
him his business, and now he is to teach our
son !"

The Colonel most conscientiously carried out
his trust, and the Prince entered upon the
routine of his duties as Captain.   The riding
lessons, the horse-breaking, the stable drill, the

gymnastic courses, the stores of his squadron,
were all handed over to his personal control and
management, and so quickly and practically did
he master the duties of a cavalry officer, that
on the 31st August, 1855, he was appointed to
command the regiment. About this time an
officer, who has since been somewhat talked of,
was appointed Aide-de-camp to the Prince ; a
man of few words, but striking lucidity of
expression and determination of character, and
an enthusiastic lover of music, whose age was
just that of the century. His name was
Colonel von Moltke, and he was at the time
Chief of the Staff of the Fourth Army Corps.

During the Summer of 1855, the Prince went
for a second time to England. Perhaps on the
occasion of his former visit, four years previously, a plan had already suggested itself to
him which he now determined to realize, of
asking the hand of the Princess Royal in
marriage. At any rate he now expressed a
wish to visit the Queen and the Prince Consort,
who invited him to stay at Balmoral ; and on
the 20th of September the Prince Consort
wrote to his old friend and confidant, Baron
Stockmar, to tell him that the proposal, made

with the concurrence of the King, as well as of
the Prince of Prussia, had been accepted, subject, of course, to the consent of the Princess
Royal herself, from whom, he added, he did not
anticipate any hesitation. It was, however,
not to be broken to her till after her Confirmation in the following Spring, and the marriage
was on no account to take place until the
Princess had passed her seventeenth birthday.
But with all these excellent dispositions the
natural impatience of the Prince prevailed, and
on the 29th of September, when the royal party
were riding unattended over the moors, a spray
of the rare white heather, which the Prince
dismounted to pluck and offer to his future
bride, drew the secret from his lips, and the
happy alliance was arranged, not by the
manœuvring of diplomacy or the scheming of
politicians, but naturally, and as in the every-
day world, by the spontaneous impulse of two
young hearts towards each other.

On his return to Bonn the Prince unburdened
his heart to Mr. Perry, whom he had from the
outset treated with the greatest confidence, and
to whom he had spoken of his hope of winning
the hand of the Princess Royal. " It was not

politics," he said, " it was not ambition ; it was
my heart."

On the 2nd of October the Prince Consort
wrote to Baron Stockmar : " Prince Frederick
William left us yesterday . . . . The young
people are genuinely in love with one another :
the guilelessness, simplicity, and unselfishness
of the young man are quite touching . . . . We
are quite unprepared for any public announcement of the marriage at present. The secret
must be kept *tout bien que mal.*"   But the
secret leaked out, as such secrets always do ;
the visits of the future Sovereign of Prussia
were too significant to be disregarded.

The engagement of Princess Louise to
the Prince Regent, now the reigning Grand
Duke of Baden, took place on the same day,
September 29, at Coblenz.   The following year
the Prince returned to England, in May, where
he was joined shortly afterwards by his future
brother-in-law, and the two Princes received
honorary degrees from the University of Ox-
ford, and were present at the festivities of
Commemoration.   In August he was for the
first time entrusted with a public mission, and
sent to represent the King of Moscow, at the

coronation of the Emperor Alexander II., who
had succeeded his father in the previous year.
On all these journeys he was accompanied by
his new Aide-de-camp, who was about this time
promoted to the rank of Major-General. The
latter has testified in his correspondence to the
remarkable natural tact and the happy faculty
of the *apropos* displayed by the Prince in
meeting and conversing with the number of
notabilities who were here for the first time
presented to him.

On the 20th of September the marriage of
Princess Louise with the Grand Duke of Baden
took place, and shortly afterwards Prince
Frederick William received the command of the
Eleventh Regiment of Infantry, which forms
part of the garrison of Breslau, in Silesia. He
had some time previously returned from his
short term of service with the Cavalry, to the
First Infantry of the Guards, and qualified
himself to take command of the regiment. No
sooner, however, had the Prince taken up his
quarters at Breslau, than another journey to
England was determined on, and the visit,
whose ostensible object was to congratulate the
Princess upon her birthday, extended over a

month. He returned by Paris, where he was
most warmly received by the Emperor
Napoleon III. and the Empress Eugénie. A
letter from the latter describing the visit is not
without its curious interest, read in the light
of subsequent events. "The Prince is a tall,
finely proportioned man, nearly a head taller
than the Emperor, smart, fair, with light
yellow moustache, a German, as Tacitus
describes them, chivalrous in manner, and with
a touch of Hamlet about him. His companion,
a General Moltke, is a gentleman of few words,
but nothing less than a dreamer; always
attentive and commanding attention, he sur-
prises you by the most striking observations.
An imposing race, these Germans. Louis says,
the race of the future. But we have not got
to that yet."

Prince Frederick William remained with his
regiment in Silesia until September, 1857,
finding time, however, in the Summer for
another visit to England. It was originally
contemplated that the marriage should take
place this year, but the health of King Frederick
William IV., who had for some time been ailing,
gave rise to considerable anxiety, and it was

D

decided to postpone it for a while. At length
the malady, which had affected the brain, was
declared to be incurable, and on the 23rd of
October the Prince of Prussia was named Regent
for three months. This term was subsequently
prolonged from time to time, and in the following year, when the King left Berlin for Italy,
the Prince Regent assumed the full responsibility of government, which he retained until
that Monarch's death. The marriage was now
definitively fixed for January 25, 1858.

It was with sincere regret that Prince
Frederick William took leave of the officers
and men of his Silesian regiment. Silesia is
the favourite province of the kingdom; the
wealthiest and most influential of the Prussian
nobility have their country seats there; the
forests offer great attractions to the sportsman;
and Breslau itself is within easy distance of
the pleasant country sloping upwards to the
giant mountains which mark the boundary of
Bohemia. Besides, he had greatly appreciated
the freedom of life which his sojourn here had
permitted, and was much attached to and beloved by the regiment he had commanded.
The close of his farewell speech was remem-

bered a few years later, when, in the campaign
of '66, he was entrusted with the command of
the Second Army, and with orders to protect
the province of Silesia : " I shall never forget
these days, nor you," he said ; " and my ardent
desire, which it would give me the greatest joy
to see accomplished, is that I may some day
receive with you—who are, for the most part,
my pupils—the baptism of blood before the
enemy."

Meanwhile, the day fixed for the wedding
ceremony drew near. On the 23rd of January,
Prince Frederick William arrived in England
to claim his bride. London had been already
several days *en fête*. On the evening of the
23rd there was a State performance at Her
Majesty's Theatre, where the Prince was, for
the first time, present during the festival pro-
ceedings, sitting beside the Princess Royal ;
and rarely has London witnessed such an enthusiastic scene. The singing of the National
Anthem was the signal for a burst of cheering, to
which the Queen graciously responded. A cry
of "Princess" then rang through the house. The
Queen beckoned the Princess Royal to the front
of the box, and there she curtseyed her acknow-

ledgments amidst a display of feeling which
made the pretty episode for ever memorable.
The wedding took place at the Chapel Royal,
St. James's, on the following Monday. The
accounts of the ceremony, read in the light
and shadow of all that has passed since, are
eminently touching from the genuine and
natural feeling evinced, and an eye-witness,
describing the scene as the procession left the
Chapel Royal, wrote : " The light of happiness
in the eyes of the bride appealed to the most
reserved among the spectators, and an audible
' *God bless you !* ' passed from mouth to mouth
along the line." The details of the ceremony,
recorded by a loving hand in the Queen's diary,
and published in Sir Theodore Martin's life of
the Prince Consort, are too well-known to call
for reproduction here. It shall only be mentioned that the wedding rings were made of
pure Silesian gold, and that the eight brides-
maids—chosen from the fairest daughters of
England—wore the emblematic white heather,
in memory of the stranger-Prince's wooing.
Throughout the country in England the day
was celebrated as a national holiday by public
rejoicings and free dinners to the poor ; and in

the evening London was a blaze of illuminations,
for the match had become thoroughly popular.
Parliament had met the proposed vote with
scarcely a dissentient voice ; and the young
Prince had won a place in the heart of the
nation, which learned to appreciate him ever
more and more as time went on.

The short honeymoon was spent at Windsor,
and the departure was fixed for the second of
February.   The farewell procession left Buckingham Palace, and proceeded by the Strand,
St. Paul's, and London Bridge, to the station
in the Kent Road, where the royal party were
to take train for Gravesend.   The Prince
Consort, with his two eldest sons, accompanied
Prince Frederick William and his bride, while
the Queen watched from the balcony of Buckingham Palace till the procession wound out of
sight.   The snow was falling fast, but they
drove in open carriages to see the last of home.
Every point of vantage along the route was
filled to overflowing, and it seemed as if the
whole nation felt keenly the sense of parting,
and had come out in its thousands to speed on
her way, with their love and kindly solicitude,
one who, though still almost a child, was leav-

ing her country for ever, to make her home in
an alien land. It is a solemn moment, hard to
realize for those who stay at home, that in
which we turn our backs for ever on the only
life we have known, and go to meet the untried
and the new, to dwell with strange faces,
different ideas and ideals, unfamiliar associations.

At Gravesend, the royal yacht, Victoria and
Albert, was waiting to receive them : and the
closing scene in England was thus described in
the *Times* of the 23rd of February :—

" In compliance with injunctions issued just before
the arrival of the royal party, there was little cheering
on the pier itself. Still, however, it could not altogether
prevent the cheers which greeted the bride, as she stood
leaning on her husband's arm. . . . Her royal husband
was, of course, received with a most marked welcome,
which he seemed to feel; though, as usual, he always
left his bride to receive the ovations offered, and
watched her every movement with the most affectionate solicitude.

"On the affecting farewell we need not dwell.
Every heart can sympathize with them, not as rulers
or princes, but as a father who parts from his eldest
child—with young brothers, who see their sister leave
them for the first time, to cast her lot for ever in a

land of strangers. The Prince Consort was grave, but composed, though the effort it cost him to maintain an appearance of serenity was visible to all. With less self-command, the Prince of Wales and Prince Alfred made little attempt to conceal their grief. . . . . As the paddles went round, the quick flashes of broad red flame through the snowstorm, followed by the sullen boom of cannon, showed that old Tilbury was at last saluting for the departure. The Prince Consort waved his hand to the Royal Bridegroom again and again, but kept his composure; but not so did the young Princes, whose grief seemed only redoubled by the tokens of farewell round them. Neither could conceal his sorrow, and neither tried to do so, but stood brushing away the tears from their eyes. . . . . On such an occasion there was not many who could resist the contagious influence of a sorrow so innocent and so sincere, and there were few who looked with dry eyes on this departure of the daughter of England."

III.

1858—1863.

III.

1858—1863.

The bride and bridegroom's journey home was one long triumphal progress. At Herbesthal, where the German frontier was first reached, Count Redern awaited them with a message of welcome from the King. At Aix-la-Chapelle; at Cologne, where they halted for the night; at Hanover, where they alighted to pay a brief visit to the King; at Magdeburg, where a second night was passed, deputations were awaiting to receive them—triumphal arches and illuminations testified the enthusiasm and loyalty of the populations. A brilliant reception was prepared for them at Potsdam, where they arrived on the 6th February; and the following day, a Sunday, was devoted to rest after their eventful journey. On Monday, the 8th, the solemn entry into the capital took place. The sixteen miles from Potsdam to the capital were traversed by road. At the Belle-vue Palace, situated in the Thiergarten, or park, about a mile from the Brandenburg Gate, the King was waiting to greet his nephew and niece. After a short interval the procession reformed, the bells rang, the canons fired salutes, and the state coach, drawn by eight horses, arrived at the Brandenburg Gate. Here the royal pair were welcomed in the name of the garrison by the venerable Field-Marshal, Count Wrangel. A detachment of the Life Guards rode before and after the carriage; while the Prince's old regiment, the Dragoons of the Guard, formed the rest of the escort. Forty out-riders and deputations from the various Guilds headed the procession; and so, between a surging mass of spectators, they passed down the Linden Avenue, the whole length of which was hung with British and Prussian flags to the old palace and its eastern extremity, where the Prince of Prussia was waiting to receive them at the foot of the great staircase. After the ceremonial introductions had been made, the Prince and Princess appeared on the balcony, to receive the homage of the people, and watch the Guilds march past. In the evening they drove through the city, where there was not a window unilluminated, and no house so poor that it had not some decoration in honour of the festal day.   It was still hard Winter in the northern city, but its welcome was warm and generous..

After a short residence in the old Schloss, a palace in the Linden Avenue, close to the opera-house, and facing the arsenal, which had been enlarged and restored for King Frederick William III., was assigned to the young couple, where they took up their abode in the early Winter, and ever after, as Crown Prince and Princess, continued to live when in Berlin. The first Summer was spent at the Prince of Prussia's country seat of Babelsberg, the home of Prince Frederick William's boyhood ; and here, at Whitsuntide, they received a hasty visit from the Prince Consort, who returned in August with the Queen.   This visit, the bright impression left by which is fully recorded in the Queen's diary, was the only one which Her Majesty was able to pay her daughter in her new home, until the sad and memorable journey of this year, when the shadow of death was already darkening its threshold, and the streets of the capital were still draped with black in mourning for the first German Emperor.

An heir to the Hohenzollern dynasty was born on the 27th of January, 1859—the reigning Emperor, William II. The apartments at Babelsberg now became too small for the extended requirements of the young household, and from henceforth the New Palace, near Potsdam, became their Summer home. And here it was that the Crown Princess, as she soon afterwards came to be called, was able to set the example of that helpful and happy country life which she had learned in England to value, so that it was not long before its simple domestic character became proverbial, and exercised a far-reaching influence. Under her fostering hand, the old formal pleasure-grounds and the neglected gardens became a pattern of taste and arrangement. In their neighbouring farm of Bornstedt the Prince himself superintended every detail, and taught himself the management of land and labour, while the dairy and the poultry-yard were the particular care of the Princess. All the inhabitants of the neighbouring villages quickly learned to

appreciate their kindly solicitude ; the sanita-
tion of dwellings, the care for the sick and
aged among their tenants, the schools, the
children's holidays, all engaged their sympathetic interest.   One of the Prince's most
striking characteristics was his love for the
people, his genuine sympathy with the humbler
walks of life.   It was his especial pleasure to
visit the village school and listen to the
children's lessons, and sometimes he would take
the teacher's place and put the questions himself. It must have been on such an occasion
that the pretty reply was given which is
recorded in the following story :—" To what
kingdom does this belong ? " the Prince had
enquired of a little girl, touching a medal sus-
pended to his chain. " To the mineral kingdom," was the answer.   " And this ? " pointing
to a flower.   " To the vegetable kingdom."
" And I myself," he asked ; to what kingdom
do I belong ? " " To the kingdom of heaven,"
was the child's reply.

Meanwhile, there were duties, and important
ones, to perform. On the day of his marriage
the Prince had been promoted to the rank of
Major-General, and when, during the Austrian

and Italian War of 1859, it was determined to
mobilize a portion of the Prussian troops, he
was appointed to command the First Infantry
Division, an appointment confirmed and made
definite on the 25th of July.   The Peace of
Villafranca brought the war to an abrupt conclusion before the Prussian mobilization was
complete, but the experience had revealed
serious defects in the existing state of the
Army, and a Commission was immediately
organized to consider the remodelling of the
entire military system.   The Prince assisted at
all the deliberations of this Commission, and
after its sittings were closed he started with
the Princess for a tour in Silesia, and, later,
paid a hasty visit to London.

The following year a daughter was born,
Princess Charlotte, now Hereditary Princess of
Saxe-Meiningen.   It was in the late Summer
of this year that the Queen and the Prince
Consort paid their last visit together to
Germany.   During their stay at Coburg their
first grandchild, the little Prince William, was
brought by his parents to be shown to his
grandparents.   A charming picture is given in
the Queen's diary of the first appearance of the

present German Emperor "in a little white dress with black bows."

The measures of reform in the military system, which the Prince Regent held to be urgent and indispensable, led to protracted discussion, and eventually to the resignation of the Liberal Ministry. The question was still undecided when, on the 2nd of January, 1861, King Frederick William IV. died, and the Prince Regent ascended the throne under the name of King William I. Prince Frederick William, who had in the previous year been promoted to the rank of Lieutenant-General, now assumed the title of Crown Prince. The Coronation took place with much pomp at Königsberg, on his birthday, the 18th of October. He was on this occasion named Protector of the ancient University of Königsberg, as successor to the late King; and shortly afterwards, in accordance with precedent, was appointed Stadtholder of Pomerania, though the formal announcement did not appear in the *Gazette* till the following year, on the birthday of Prince William, the reigning Emperor, when it was couched in these terms:—"I have appointed your Royal Highness to be Stadt-

E

holder of Pomerania, and desire thus to mark the day, on which so happy an event in the history of our family is commemorated, by an especial token of my fatherly affection.— WILLIAM."

Early in the married life of the Crown Prince and Princess fell the shadow of those domestic sorrows which darkened so many of their years. On March 16th, 1861, the Duchess of Kent died; and the loss of "this much-loved grandmother" was soon to be followed by a still nearer and more untimely bereavement. It was not long after the festivities of the Coronation that the health of the Prince Consort began to give cause for anxiety. It had been his special desire that the Crown Princess, who had herself been suffering in health, should not expose herself to the risk of a Winter journey, and she was therefore not present at that sad event which has cast a permanent gloom over the British Court. Needless to say, the Crown Prince crossed to England immediately, to be of such service as he might, and to attend the funeral of one to whom he had looked up with fond affection; a guide and a counsellor, whose moderation and political foresight he never ceased to regard with respect and veneration. Some months later, in the Spring of the following year, he was once more in England, to attend, at the special desire of the Queen, the opening of the second great International Exhibition, for which he was Prussian Commissioner. A few days afterwards he was the guest of the Royal Academy at their annual banquet, and in his speech on that occasion he naturally referred to the loss which had cast a gloom over the festivities, and recalled the debt that was owed to the initiator of those international gatherings which have done so much to promote the interests of commerce, and, by teaching the nations to know one another better, have so largely contributed to their peace and welfare. This speech, which later on in the evening was characterized by Lord Granville as "a speech remarkable for its simple and truthful eloquence, and which, by a touch of feeling concerning one of whom this country is proud, went directly to our hearts," was as follows :—

"SIR CHARLES EASTLAKE, YOUR ROYAL HIGHNESS, MY LORDS AND GENTLEMEN,—I hope that the gratitude which I feel for the cordiality with which you have been pleased to propose and receive my health will not be measured by the manner in which I return thanks for it, as I am sorry to say I fear I shall not be able to express my feelings as I should perhaps be able to do were I longer accustomed to the language of this dear country. I thank you first for the way in which you have been kind enough to speak of my near relationship to the Royal Family of England; nor can I on such an occasion omit referring to the loss which this country has recently sustained—a loss felt so intimately by your Royal Family and also by my own. We have all heard from the President how that loss has been felt here, and I am happy to say that in my own country the same monumental feeling will always remain associated with the memory of that dear Prince who was taken so suddenly from us.

"It is not necessary for me to say how happy I am to be able to be present at this great festival of peace, and at the same time to honour the great undertaking which we owe to the master-mind of him I was so proud to regard as my father-in-law. I have also, Sir Charles, to thank you for the manner in which you spoke just now of the state of Art and Science in my own country, and especially of the articles sent to the Great International Exhibition. I am happy to think, from the way in which that reference of the President was received, that you all appear to agree with him on that point, and I hope I can say that the same feeling for English art is reciprocated by my country. Perhaps

I may be allowed to say, as I am proud to say, that the Princess Royal of your country is one of the first representatives of English art in my country. Returning thanks again for the kind way in which I have been received, I can only add that I hope it will be a new tie, strengthening those warm sympathies I have always felt for this great country; and, more than this, that the strong sympathy which always existed in my own heart will in Prussia and the great Fatherland of Germany be more and more, and for ever, retained." *

No mean achievement in a foreign tongue. Among the guests at this Academy banquet, of which the Crown Prince ever preserved a pleasant recollection, were Thackeray and Dickens, the latter of whom responded on behalf of Literature.

A few months later, the Crown Prince was again at Königsberg, where he was solemnly invested with the office of High Protector of the University, which he had consented to fill at the time of the Coronation. His speech on this occasion must also be quoted, for in it the aims and aspirations which were ever nearest to his heart found expression :

"I looked upon the inheritance to which I have

* *Times*, May 5, 1862.

succeeded as a renewed invitation to contribute my aid
to the development of Art and Science. That which my
ancestors have established and honourably maintained
will be sacred no less to me their successor; and I
promise, on my part, to support and extend the
establishment by all the means in my power. I have
in my mind those great names which have made this
University illustrious—above all, the name of one
man, whose teachings have gone forth far over the
bounds of our German Fatherland, and have enlightened
the whole round world.*   I have myself been a member
of an University, and I know the spirit by which it is
animated. The work of the Universities—the development of the mind and the strengthening of character—
is a noble work, in that they fulfil this mission, not
only for the advancement of learning, but in the service
of the State. Thanks to the spirit which fires the
youth of Germany, I count upon her students under-
standing and appreciating the greatness of this work."

During this Summer, there was consolation
in the house of mourning; a second son was
born, Prince Henry, who has become the sailor-
Prince of Germany. In the meanwhile, the
conflict between the Government and the
Chambers had continued, and was now
assuming a more acute phase, when in Sep-

* Kant.

tember, 1862, the King called upon Herr von
Bismarck to take the reins of Government in
hand.

From this period began for Prussia that
wonderful career of success, the extraordinary
decade which culminated with the declaration
of the German Empire at Versailles.   Of the
relation of the Crown Prince to political life it
does not enter into the design of the present
sketch to speak ; but it may here be placed on
record that through the quarter of a century
which followed, he never broke the rule he had
laid down for himself to refrain from any
open expression of opinion, and from taking any
active part in political life.   Differences of
opinion there must always be, and the younger
generation is not always patient of the views
and methods of the older.   But whatever may
have been the feelings and sentiments of the
Crown Prince himself, he cheerfully and
loyally carried out the arduous duties which it
fell to him to perform ; and, at a subsequent
date, when called upon for a time to assume
the Regency, he faithfully followed in the lines
that were laid down for him.   It argues no
slight strength of character, and a paramount

sense of duty, to have so faithfully appreciated
and conquered the difficulties of the position
which it was his lot to fill.

The Crown Prince and the Princess spent
the Winter months of this year in a long tour
through Italy, during which an improvised
expedition was made to Tunis and Malta.
They had joined the Prince of Wales on the
Royal yacht " Osborne," and at Naples celebrated his coming of age on board, returning
subsequently to Rome, where they took up
their abode in the Palazzo Caffarelli.

IV.

1864—1869.

IV.

1864—1869.

WHEN the Danish War broke out in 1864 the
Crown Prince had no military command, but
was attached to the Staff of Field-Marshal
Count von Wrangel, who had the chief command
of the united Austrian and Prussian armies.
His task was to be one of conciliation. The
allied armies were the allies of circumstance
rather than of sympathy, and the rivalry of the
commanding officers, the jealousy of the troops,
could hardly fail to produce a feeling of friction
which might, if not counteracted with tact and
authority, have prejudiced the prospects of the
campaign. In all such differences and disputes
the Crown Prince formed the court of reference,
and the fact that the cessation of hostilities was
so soon afterwards followed by the outbreak
of the Austrian and Prussian War proves how

difficult must have been the task imposed upon
him, and how effectual was the influence of his
tact and judgment in preventing these dis-
agreements from assuming an acute phase
before the war was brought to a successful
conclusion. At a skirmish before Düppel he
was for the first time under fire, and he assisted
at the storming of the lines of Düppel on the
18th of April, 1864. Throughout the severe
Winter campaign he shared every hardship with
the troops ; he was continually in their midst,
and the sight of his familiar figure, in the long
military paletot, with his short pipe in his
mouth, was a signal for general enthusiasm.
It was now that the Crown Prince, in co-operation with the Crown Princess, who had gone
to meet him at Hamburg as soon as the
fighting was over, founded the first of those
institutions for the relief of the victims of war,
of which many were called into existence later,
in the stormy days which were yet in store for
Prussia. After the conclusion of Peace the
Crown Prince was entrusted with the command
of the Second Army Corps, which he retained
until the war of 1870. On the 11th of September of the same year Prince Sigismund was

born, "a great source of rejoicing to his parents." The history of the family of Hohenzollern is full of strange coincidences, but perhaps there are few stranger than that connected with the brief life of this little Prince, ushered into the world after the declaration of peace, with the Emperor of Austria for his godfather, to be taken away once more, almost on the very day his native land had drawn the sword against Austria.

The interval of peace was short. Since the Italian war of 1859 the relations between Austria and Prussia had continued strained, and the Danish campaign had only served to widen the breach. The struggle for the hegemony of the German Confederation was at hand. Austria realized at length that Prussia was in deadly earnest, and meant not only to oust her from the headship she still claimed, but from the confederation altogether; and long before appeal was made to the decision of the sword, rumours of war were rife, and hostile preparations continued. In May, 1866, the Prussian army was mobilized. The fighting strength of the kingdom was divided into three armies, of which the second was placed under

the command of the Crown Prince, with orders
to protect the province of Silesia, of which he
was appointed Military Governor during the
mobilization.

So long as war still hung in the balance, the
Crown Prince used his influence on the side of
conciliation, and did all that was in his power
to avert a conflict. Now that it appeared
inevitable, he was as ever ready to do his duty.
A few days after the christening of his second
daughter, who, having been baptized on the
24th of May, received the name of Victoria, he
rejoined his Staff at Breslau; and, as the veteran
generals gathered round him, he said, with his
genial smile: "It really is too bad that so
young a man as I am should command you,
with all your experience, and I with none
myself." On the 14th of June the Prussian
proposals were rejected in the Diet at Frankfort; Hanover and Hesse fell almost without a
struggle, before the iron will of the great
minister, and the dogs of war were loosed.
The day after the issue of the Royal proclamation to the Army, the Crown Prince
addressed his troops from his headquarters at
Neisse :—

" Soldiers of the Second Army,

"You have heard the words of our King and Commander-in-Chief. The efforts of His Majesty to preserve peace for our country have been vain. With a heavy heart, but relying on the devotion and bravery of his army, the King has resolved to fight for the honour and independence of Prussia, and for the effectual reorganization of Germany.

"Placed at your head by the grace of my royal father, and thanks to the confidence he reposes in me, I am proud, as our King's first subject, to stake my life with you for all that our fatherland holds most sacred.

"Soldiers! For the first time in the last fifty years our army has to face a foe that is its equal match. Have confidence in your strength, in the efficiency of your arms, and remember we have now got to beat the same enemy whom our greatest King once vanquished with a little army.

"And now forward, under the old Prussian device,
        'With God for king and country!'"

The Crown Prince had left for the campaign under very painful circumstances, for a few days before his departure, Prince Sigismund, 'a beautiful boy, the joy and pride of his parents,' was taken very ill. Even the doctor who had attended him was summoned to the front by the fate of war, and the Crown

Princess was left alone with her sick child. The illness, which was at first difficult to recognize, assumed a fatal form,* and on the 18th of June the little Prince succumbed, leaving his mother well-nigh distracted and alone, without anyone to share her sorrow. The news reached the Crown Prince just as the army was on the point of advancing. He had with him one tried and trusted friend, Captain Mischke, a companion of his early days, and it was his warm sympathy on which the Crown Princess relied to help her husband at this critical moment to bear so hard and crushing a blow.

There were perhaps many others in the camp who had their silent troubles ; such things must always be. It is not the least of the terrors of war, that, when the summons comes, the claims of home and the affections of the individual must yield to the general welfare ; but it may have encouraged some of those who stood in like case to see how bravely and unswervingly their leader went about his duty, never allowing his private griefs for a moment to divert his energies from the grave

* Meningitis cerebralis.

task he had in hand. Those who knew him
well were aware how acutely he suffered, but it
was only after the war was over, in a speech
made to the Municipality of Berlin, when ten-
dering their congratulations on his safe return,
that he spoke of his personal loss : " It was a
heavy trial," he said, " to be separated from my
wife and my dying boy ; that I could not be
there to close his eyes. Hard as it was at the
time to have to be far from my home and family,
I can now look back upon it with satisfaction,
for it was a sacrifice which I offered to my
country."

The force commanded by the Crown Prince
consisted of four army corps ; the first under
General von Bonin, the fifth under General
von Steinmetz, who was commander of the First
Army in the war of 1870, the sixth under
General von Mutius, and the Corps of the
Guards, under Prince August of Würtemberg.
He was supported by an able adviser in the
person of General von Blumenthal, who acted
as Chief of the Staff. General von Blumenthal
accompanied the Prince in the same capacity
during the Franco-German war, and one of the
few public acts of his brief reign was to bestow

F

a field-marshal's bâton on this old friend and
faithful servant, for whose military capacity and
private character he had unbounded esteem,
which it was his especial pleasure to express
whenever he had an opportunity.

The instructions issued by General von
Moltke, who as chief of the head-quarter Staff
directed the operations of the three armies,
were : to enter Bohemia through the passes of
the Giant Mountains, and effect a junction with
the armies of Prince Frederick Charles and
General Herwarth. A wide latitude was however left to the judgment and initiative of the
commander, and it was pointed out that, if
their concentration was not yet effected, circumstances might admit of a series of attacks
in overwhelming force on isolated bodies of the
enemy, which might modify the scheme of
campaign. The junction of the armies in the
direction of Gitschin was however still to be
the ultimate object, and the relative positions
of the three armies was ever to be kept in
sight, with a view to mutual support. This
forecast was carried out in its double event.
Four Austrian corps operating independently
opposed the invading Prussians; with the

exception of a slight check experienced by
General von Bonin on the 27th, a series of
rapid successes between the 26th and 28th
cleared the way into Bohemia, and on the 30th
the three advancing Prussian corps re-united
with the sixth, which had formed the rear-
guard. On the 1st of July the Crown Prince
issued the following proclamation :—

" Only a few days have elapsed since we crossed the
Bohemian frontier, and a series of brilliant victories has
marked our advance, and ensured the attainment of
our first object, to hold the passages of the Elbe, and
unite with the First Army.

" The gallant Fifth Army Corps, under its heroic
leader (General v. Steinmetz), has gloriously repulsed
on three successive days as many fresh bodies of the
enemy advancing against them. The Guards have
been twice engaged, and have brilliantly succeeded in
beating the enemy back. The First Army Corps has
displayed the greatest bravery under the most trying
circumstances.

" Five flags, two standards, 8,000 prisoners have
fallen into our hands, and many thousands of killed and
wounded, are evidence of how severe the losses of the
enemy have been.

" We have to mourn the loss of many gallant comrades, killed or wounded, who have made a gap in our

F 2

ranks. But the thought of having fallen for their
King and their country, together with the consciousness of victory, will have afforded consolation to the
dying and comfort to the suffering.

"God grant that we may continue in our career of
victory!

"I thank the generals, officers, and men of the
Second Army for their gallantry in battle, and for
their patience in surmounting the great difficulties we
have had to encounter, and I feel proud to command
such troops."

But the hardest struggle was yet to come.
The First Army and the Army of the Elbe had
also in the meantime entered Bohemia, and
after a series of successes had converged upon
Gitschin, the point at which the three armies
were to effect their union. The King arrived
at Gitschin on the 2nd of July to take over the
supreme command. It was decided that the
troops should enjoy a short rest before the
decisive engagement with the forces of General
Benedek, now concentrated in the neighbourhood of Königgrätz; but a message from Prince
Frederick Charles, who was not aware of the
full strength of General Benedek's army, that
he should attack the Austrian position on the

following morning. relying on the support of
the Second Army and the Army of the Elbe.
changed these dispositions, and the general
attack was ordered for the 3rd. The Crown
Prince's army was still some fourteen miles
from Gitschin. and on the night of the 2nd
orders were despatched for his immediate
advance. On the safe delivery of these orders
hung the issue of the day. An hour after
midnight. Count Finkenstein started on his
eventful ride through the enemy's country,
while a second instruction was forwarded by a
safe and more circuitous route. At a quarter
past three on the morning of the third he
reached the bivouack of the advance-guard of
the Second Army, and warned General von
Bonin to be prepared. By four in the morning
the message was safely delivered at head-
quarters. and by daybreak the columns were
advancing without train or baggage, straining
every nerve to reach the field in time. The
Crown Prince rode at their head. urging and
encouraging his men. as they heard in the
distance the thunder of the cannon of Sadowa
growing nearer and nearer. The Prussians
were heavily outnumbered in the morning, and

victory hung in the scales. The Austrians
fought, as ever, with the utmost bravery and
determination, and had the Crown Prince
reached the battlefield a little later the whole
issue of the war might have been changed.
But it was only one o'clock when the artillery
of the Second Army opened fire upon the
Austrian right, by two o'clock the whole army
was engaged, and General von Moltke, turning
to the King, said, "Now, no power on earth
can take the victory from your Majesty." It
was the forced march of the Second Army that
won the decisive battle of Sadowa. The
Austrians lost in killed, wounded, and prisoners,
upwards of 40,000 men, while the rest of their
army was in full retreat over the Elbe or into
the fortress of Königgrätz.

It was late in the evening before the Crown
Prince found his father. Their meeting is thus
recorded in his diary : " At last, after much
questioning and searching, we met the King ;
I reported to him the presence of my army on
the field of battle, and kissed his hand, and he
embraced me. For a time neither of us could
find words. At last he said that he was
rejoiced at my successes, and that I had shown

aptitude for command. He had confered on me, as I would know by telegraph, the Order 'le Mérite.' I had not received this telegram ; and so my father and Sovereign bestowed upon me, on the field of a battle which I had assisted in winning, our highest Order of military distinction. I was deeply moved, and those who assisted at the interview seemed to share my emotion."

The interview was thus also briefly described by the King in a letter written on the following morning to the Queen. " At last I met Fritz with his Staff, quite late, at eight o'clock. What a moment after all we had gone through, and on the evening of such a day ! I gave him myself the Order ' Pour le Mérite.' Tears started from his eyes, for he had not received my telegram announcing it. It was a complete surprise."

The Order " Pour le Mérite " is so highly esteemed, because it can only be won for personal gallantry upon the field of battle, and it had an especial value for the Prince to whom so many decorations had fallen *ex officio*, in being the one Order which had to be earned. By the express desire of the Emperor William, this

Order, which he had won himself in 1815, was hung round his neck after death, and buried with him.

The war was not over, but there was little more fighting for the Second Army to do. The Prussian troops pressed on to within sight of Vienna, and on the 26th of July preliminaries of peace were signed at Nikolsburg. The Treaty of Prague, signed in the following month, prepared the way for the unity of Germany. The immediate results were that the Sovereign of Prussia, whose territories had now been extended by the annexation of Hanover, Hesse, Schleswig-Holstein, Nassau, and Frankfort, became President of a new North German Confederation, including all the States of Northern and Central Germany, with absolute control of their military organization, while offensive and defensive alliances with the States and Southern Germany placed at his disposal the whole available fighting strength of the German nation.

Such were the momentous changes effected by the brief but brilliant campaign of 1866, to whose success the Crown Prince had so largely contributed. As he drove into Berlin beside

the King, on the 4th of August, and the people
closed in round the carriage with cheer on
cheer, he may well have felt a thrill of conscious
pride at having so fully justified the high command with which he had been entrusted.   The
glory of the successful soldier is still man's
fondest ambition ; we had nearly all of us rather
have been Cæsar than Socrates.   But the
scenes of the last weeks had left a dark impression on the quick sensibilities and the
gentle nature of the soldier-Prince, which the
flush of triumph could not altogether efface,
and he had seen upon what narrow issues the
fate of battles hung.   There was still much
more of this rough work for him to do, inevitable for the Prince as for the Private.   But
his inmost feelings are revealed in a few words
which he made use of sometime afterwards in
the course of conversation, when the Luxemburg question was agitating the public mind,
and the danger of hostilities was again within measurable distance.   " You have never seen
war," he said to one who had lightly spoken of
its probability, " or you would never pronounce
that word so calmly.   I, who have been
brought face to face with war, must tell you

that it is a paramount duty to avoid it, if it be possible. To make war is to incur a terrible responsibility. A statesman, even when he foresees the necessity of war, ought not to provoke it by artificial means, unless he be a genius and is confident of success. Otherwise he is tempting God. On the other hand, to await the contingency of war with firmness, and not to shrink from it if it is forced upon one, is the duty of a man. In acting so, we shall have public opinion and Heaven on our side."

After the war of 1866 the Crown Prince rejoined the Crown Princess in Haringsdorf, a little village on the shores of the Baltic, to which the Princess and her children had retired on account of the cholera, which was then very bad in Potsdam. Thence they proceeded to Admannsdorf, in Silesia, not far from the Bohemian frontier, where the Princess occupied herself in tending the wounded soldiers, both Prussian and Austrian.

And now once more it fell to his lot to undertake the task of conciliation, and to gain the attachment of the new provinces ; and as he travelled from one to the other, inspecting their

troops or visiting their cities, his influence was
ever at work, to temper the mortifications of
surrender, by raising the ideal of an united
Fatherland, and by his personal charm and
genial manner to reveal to them in the representative of Prussia a friend, and not a
conqueror. As his heart naturally went out to
all men, and as he had a real and strong
affection for all Germans, to whatever state
they belonged, the part he had to play was a
very welcome one. Moreover, as he had
entered the campaign with a heavy heart,
though fully convinced of its necessity, he
never ceased subsequently to do all that was
in his power to restore the natural bond
between Austrians and Prussians, and remove
the traces of their temporary estrangement.

Notwithstanding the ominous development
of the Luxemburg question, and the tension
with France, which never wholly subsided after
the Treaty of Prague, the next few years were
spent in peace, and the Crown Prince resumed
his command of the Second Army Corps. At
the end of 1866 he was once more in Russia, for
the marriage of the Cesarevitch, and in the
following year he visited the Paris Exhibition

with the Crown Princess. While they were
there King William also arrived, and for a while
it seemed as if these visits had succeeded in
dispelling somewhat the feeling of mistrust
between the neighbour nations. In 1868 the
Crown Prince went to Turin. to be present at
the marriage of Prince Humbert. The latter
had been in Berlin the previous year, and with
this visit renewed the acquaintance the two
Princes had formed in Milan some years
previously, and strengthened that cordial
friendship between the future rulers of Germany and Italy which continued unbroken to
the last. Their positions were not altogether
dissimilar. The making of Italy was as yet
only partially accomplished, but the campaign
of 1866 had greatly lightened the task of King
Victor Emmanuel and Cavour. In every Italian
city which was visited by the Crown Prince
enthusiastic demonstrations testified how sen-
sible the populations were to the debt they owed
to Germany. The martial bearing and the
winning manner of the hero of Sadowa appealed
directly to the warm temperament of the Italian
people, who gave him a Southern welcome, and
it was a source of unmixed pleasure to the Royal

traveller to find that he had won the love of a
people whose land he loved so well. Among
the many personal friends of the Crown Prince
in Italy may be mentioned the celebrated
Statesmen, Marco Minghetti, Giovanni Morelli,
and Count Robilant.

In the same year, the Wedding day of Queen
Victoria and Prince Albert, and the anniversary
of the Princess Royal's christening, was marked
by another conspicuous event in the family of
the Crown Prince. A fourth son was born,
who seemed sent to fill the sad gap which the
death of his little brother had made two years
before. The present Emperor of Russia was
sponsor to Prince Waldemar, and the christening took place on the Emperor William's
seventy-first birthday, at Berlin. He was a
child of unusual promise, who inherited all the
brightness of his father's nature, with that
physical beauty which is so often the privilege
of those whom the gods love. His little life
was long enough to win the hearts of all who
were brought near him, and his early death, in
his eleventh year, left a gap which could never
be filled. It was by the side of this much-loved
child that the father chose his last resting-place,

when the great tragedy which the passing year
has witnessed drew to its close.

In November, 1869, the Sovereigns of all the
Maritime Powers were invited to take part in
the ceremonious opening of the Suez Canal;
and this invitation afforded the Crown Prince,
who was deputed to represent the King, an
opportunity of realizing the long-cherished
plan of a journey through the East. Pausing
on his way to make a pilgrimage to Dante's
grave at Ravenna, he crossed from Brindisi by
Corfu to Corinth. From Athens he sailed to
Constantinople, where the Sultan made over to
his guest the concession of an ancient monastery
of the Knights of St. John in Jerusalem, which
was to furnish the site for a German Protestant
Church and hospital. Embarking thence, he
arrived on the 3rd of November at Jaffa, and,
escorted by a detachment of Marines from the
Hertha, started at once for the Holy City,
which was reached on the following day, after
a night in camp at Bab-el-Wady. Jerusalem is
now no longer the goal of pilgrims from the
Catholic countries of Europe; but Greeks and
Armenians still make their way in numbers to
the Holy Sepulchre, and they were a motley

throng of all the peoples of the East that lined
the narrow streets to witness the Prince's entry.
As ever, full of consideration for all about him,
he turned to the Marines in his escort, and
bade them keep close to him, that they might
not miss any of the sights.   The deep impression made by the haunting spirit of a spot so
familiar through long and tender association,
found record in the following entry in the diary
in which he never failed to chronicle his observations and experiences :—

" I shall never, as long as I live, forget that first
evening in Jerusalem, when I saw the sunset from the
Mount of Olives, and that wondrous peace of Nature
supervened which even in any other place has a solemn
character of its own.   Here the spirit could lift itself
over earthly things, and dwell uninterruptedly in those
thoughts which move the heart of every Christian when
he looks back on that great work of redemption, which
found upon this hallowed spot its loftiest expression.
To read over again one's favourite passages in the
Gospels at such a place is in itself an act of worship."

From Jerusalem, Bethlehem and the graves
of the Patriarchs were visited, and after a brief
excursion to Lebanon and Damascus the Crown
Prince   re-embarked   for   Port   Said.   The

ceremonies connected with the opening of the Suez Canal were over in time to enable him to reach the first cataract of the Nile, and even to penetrate some distance into Nubia, before rejoining the Crown Princess and his family for the Christmas rejoicing at Cannes, where they had been staying with Princess Alice, whose husband had accompanied the Crown Prince on his travels. The last days of the year were spent at Paris, where the Emperor Napoleon paid them a visit at their hotel. They were " struck by finding him changed and ailing and much dejected." In the course of conversation the Emperor mentioned that he had appointed a new Minister, M. Ollivier. Thence, on the morning of the New Year, little anticipating what eventful days it was to bring him, the Crown Prince returned to Berlin. Before that year was over he met the Emperor Napoleon once again—the morning after the capitulation of Sedan.

V.

1870—1871.

G

V.

1870—1871.

THE Spring and early Summer of 1870 had passed uneventfully; the Crown Prince had been sent by his doctors for a cure to Carlsbad, from which he returned in April: and the only event which had marked the year with importance in his family was the birth of a daughter, Princess Sophie, on the 14th of June. The King had gone to Ems, as was his annual habit, when suddenly the crisis came, and the war which had so long been anticipated took Europe by surprise. This is not a place to enter into the causes, immediate or remote, which led to the eventful struggle, nor is any detailed description contemplated of that memorable campaign. So much only will be dealt with in the following pages as may serve to throw light upon the military genius

and character of the subject of the present
sketch.

After his well-known interview with M.
Benedetti, the King returned immediately to
Berlin.   He was met at Brandenburg by the
Crown   Prince.   Both   appreciated   the   full
gravity of the moment and the issues that were
at stake ; for now, if ever, the question of an
united Germany was to be finally decided, and
Prussia was to triumph or to disappear.   All
along the route two private secretaries had
been constantly occupied in deciphering the
telegraphic messages which were handed in at
every station ; and it was on the King's arrival
at Berlin that the Crown Prince read to him,
by the flickering light of a gas-jet in the
station waiting-room, a despatch from Paris
announcing the stormy meeting in the French
chambers, which clearly indicated the condition
of the public mind in Paris.   It was to be war ;
and the King on learning its contents simply
said : " I think I can only answer this message
by ordering the mobilization of the whole
German army, and in half an hour I shall be
ready to sign the necessary papers."   The gas-
lamp by which the eventful message was read

was afterwards taken from its place and retained as a cherished relic.

The plan of campaign had long been prepared, and all went forward with order and precision. On the 19th of July the French Chargé d'Affairs at Berlin handed in the declaration of war, and the whole fighting strength of Germany was already mobilizing and streaming to the Rhine. The King assumed the supreme command of the united German Army, while General Moltke, as Chief of the Staff, accompanied his head-quarters, and directed the military operations. The available forces were divided into three armies. The first, commanded by General von Steinmitz, was ordered to concentrate on the Moselle, in the neighbourhood of Treves. The second was placed under the command of Prince Frederick Charles, whose head-quarters were first fixed at Mayence, and directed to press forward to the frontier. The Third Army, which was to concentrate on the Upper Rhine, and to form the left, or southern wing, was similarly to advance across the frontier, keeping up close communication with the centre. It was commanded by the Crown Prince. His

Chief of the Staff was General von Blumenthal ; the Artillery were under the orders of Lieutenant-General Herckt, and the Engineers under Major-General Schulz. The Crown Prince was well fitted, both by his character and his rank, to assume the difficult task of leading and conciliating the various elements of which the Third Army was composed. At least a dozen different dialects of German were spoken in its ranks. It consisted of the two Bavarian Army Corps, the combined Corps of Baden and Würtemberg, and the Fifth, Sixth, and Eleventh Prussian Army Corps, with the Second and Fourth Cavalry divisions, amongst which might be found Westphalians, Hessians, and Thuringians, with the regiments from Waldeck and Frankfort.

On the 25th of July, the christening of Princess Sophie took place. It was an anxious party that met round the baptismal font, for there were few present there who were not under orders for the front. The gentlemen were already in their high boots and campaigning accoutrements. Emotion, anxiety, and excitement made the King

unable to hold his little grandaughter at the
baptismal font. according to wont. and he
deputed the task to the Queen Augusta.
On the 25th, the Crown Prince once more
went to church, and received the Communion
with the Princess, and early on the morning
of the 26th he departed without taking
leave; he wished to spare his wife the agony
of parting. He first proceeded to Munich,
to pay a hasty visit to the King of Bavaria.
The reception accorded him wherever he
showed himself, the enthusiasm which greeted
his appearance by the side of the young
King in the theatre. augured well for the
spirit of the Bavarian troops. Proceeding
from Munich to Stuttgart, he paused on
his way at Ingoldstadt to introduce himself
as their commander to the assembled officers
of the Bavarian Army, and addressed them
in the following words : " I cannot sufficiently
express to you the honour which I feel has
been done me by your King in entrusting
his army to my command. Let us not
conceal from ourselves that we have before
us a momentous struggle, but the universal
enthusiasm which we are witnesses of

from every corner of Germany bids me hope
that, with God's help, it will be a victorious
struggle, which will lead at last to a peace that
shall crown our German Fatherland with prosperity. Let us then rely on our good cause,
upon our good sword!" By Stuttgardt and
Carlsruhe he proceeded to Spires, where his
head-quarters were first established, and at once
began that difficult task, which it is his special
merit to have carried through so successfully,
of consolidating his army, morally as well as
practically, and welding its many elements into
one harmonious whole. On the day of his
arrival, the 30th, he was in the camp of the
Bavarians, observing, encouraging, asking a
friendly question of this man and that, and
spreading by his genial presence, that contagious enthusiasm which is worth so much on
the eve of battle. The same day he issued his
Proclamation to the Army :—

    "Soldiers of the Third Army,

        "Appointed by my royal father Com-
mander-in-Chief of the Third Army, I greet the troops
of Prussia, Bavaria, Würtemberg, and Baden, who are
henceforth under my command. It fills me with pride
and satisfaction to be advancing against the foe at the

head of an army composed of men from every part of our common German Fatherland, for the national cause, for the right, for the honour of Germany. We are marching to a great and grave struggle, but convinced of the justice of our cause, and relying on your bravery, your endurance, and your manliness, we have no misgivings as to its victorious issue. Therefore let us hold fast to our true brotherhood in arms, that with God's help we may unroll our banners to new victories for the glory and the peace of our united Fatherland.

"FREDERICK WILLIAM,

"Crown Prince of Prussia."

On the 3rd of August the Prince pushed on his head-quarters to Landau, and issued orders that on the following day his troops should cross the Lauter, and enter hostile territory. Reconnaissances had proved that the French showed no disposition to strike the first blow, and the fact that the frontier lines were still unoccupied, justified the presumption that they were not yet fully prepared. The Seventh French Corps d'Armée, under General Félix Douay, detailed to protect the Southern passes of the Vosges, which was the first to come to close quarters with the Third Army, had been the last to complete its mobilization, and the

General was quite unprepared to carry out an instruction despatched on the 27th of July to join the division of Marshal MacMahon, whose troops were concentrated near Strasburg. The stragetic plan of the Emperor Napoleon to unite the armies of Metz and Strasburg, to cross the Rhine with an overwhelming force and occupy Baden and the Palatinate, was anticipated by the rapidity of the German mobilization and advance.

As day broke on the morning of the 4th the Crown Prince advanced on Weissenburg. The town itself, situated on the river Lauter, was fortified with obsolete ramparts dating from the last century, but the heights to the south-west, known as the Geisburg, afforded a very strong position, and were occupied by General Douay with eleven battalions of infantry and four batteries of artillery. The Crown Prince arrived on the field of battle at a quarter past nine, and directed operations in person. Before midday the town was in the hands of the Germans, and what remained of the garrison their prisoners. The whole attack was then concentrated on the Geisberg. Many of the regiments had been as much as

eight hours on the march. but their determined
advance carried all before it, and the French,
who were heavily outnumbered, abandoned
their positions one by one.   A stubborn resistance was made in the *Schloss*, with its out-
houses, crowning the summit, and a first
attempt to carry the position by storm was
repulsed : but still new troops succeeded.   The
French, with great coolness, reserved their fire
till the enemy was within certain range, and
then opened a deadly hail from every point
of vantage.   The colours of the Seventh Royal
Grenadiers, who led the advancing column,
were passed from hand to hand, as one by one
the bearers were shot down.   At length a
battery was brought to bear upon the stronghold, now surrounded on every side by the
Prussian and Bavarian troops, and towards
one o'clock the survivors surrendered, and the
first battle of the war was won.

The victorious regiments were drawn up on
the heights as the Crown Prince rode up the
bloody slopes of the Geisberg, where the dead
and wounded were lying on every side, in
evidence of the severity of the struggle.   On
his way he paused here and there to speak

to a wounded soldier, and then standing still in the midst of his young troops, still black with powder-smoke and soiled with the dust of battle, he addressed a few stirring words of gratitude to each and all for their steadiness and gallantry. The tattered flag of the Royal Grenadiers was brought him, and he kissed it, and embraced the wounded commander of the regiment, Major von Kaisenberg, who had fallen at the head of the storming column, with the colours in his hand. Then, learning that General Douay had fallen in the battle, he desired to be shown the body of this distinguished officer. The Crown Prince went in alone to the peasant's cottage where he lay; it was a moving and suggestive sight; in the morning their chances were equal; in the flush of victory, the pathetic contrast of this brave man's fate now touched him deeply; not a soul of all the thousands he had commanded was watching at his side, only his dog sat whining by the corpse.

The German troops had undoubtedly out-numbered the French considerably. Some sixteen battalions had been engaged on their side, while the division of General Douay

numbered less than 9,000 men ; but the
strength of the French position had more
than compensated for the inequality of
numbers, and the steadiness and determination shown by the Germans had been exem-
plary.   Besides, the first ordeal had been
successfully overcome; Prussians and Bavarians
had conquered side by side. The importance
of the victory could scarcely be over-estimated,
but it was dearly bought, for ninety-one officers
and upwards of 1,400 men were left on the
battlefield.

In the afternoon of the 4th head-quarters
were advanced to Schweighofen, and on the
following day to Sulz, some seven miles from
the village of Wörth.   The news of the
defeat of his advance-guard reached Marshal
MacMahon the same evening at Strasburg.
He at once pushed forward with all the forces
he could muster, to retrieve, if possible, the
disaster, by covering the passes of the Vosges,
and attempting to drive the invading army
back over the Alsatian frontier.   With this
object he took up a strong position, on the 5th,
along a line of wooded heights to the west of
the village of Wörth, in communication with

the more distant fortress of Bitsch. In the
rear of his position lay Reichshofen, connected
with Wörth by a high road ; to the north-east
was the village of Froschweiler, to the south
Elsasshausen. the left and right centres of the
French lines, the extreme right extending as
far as Mörsbrunn, and the extreme left to
Neuweiler, in the direction of Bitsch. The
attack was expected on the 7th, and it had
been the intention of the Commander of the
Third Army to postpone the decisive encounter
till that day, when he would have been able to
bring all his five army corps into action simultaneously ; but during the night of the 5th,
and in the early morning of the 6th, a lively
interchange of shots took place between the
French outposts and the advance guard of the
Fifth Prussian Corps in the centre, and the
Second Bavarian Corps on the right. The
General in command of the Fifth Corps,
noticing considerable movement in the French
lines about 4 a.m., was under the impression
that they were about to retreat from their
positions, and ordered a reconnaissance in force.
From this reconnaissance the decisive battle
developed itself; for though orders were

despatched to the various commanders to avoid bringing on a general action at present, matters had already gone too far to make this course practicable, and the French had assumed the offensive. The commander of the Eleventh Corps, which formed the left of the first line, seeing the Fifth Corps and the Bavarians engaged, prepared to render assistance, and by midday all three corps were fully employed. At half-past twelve, the Crown Prince and his Staff arrived on the field of battle, and about the same time the First Bavarian Corps and the Würtemburg division, which had had upwards of ten miles to march that morning, were drawing into line, while the Baden regiments were following hard behind.

The first object of the Crown Prince was to drive the French out of Wörth, and having done this, to move forward and contest the positions held by the left wing of Marshal MacMahon's army, extending in a north-easterly direction to Froschweiler, while a simultaneous movement was to be directed against the French right at Elsasshausen, to prevent the possibility of their attacking the Fifth Prussian Corps in flank.

Immediately after the arrival of the Commander-in-Chief, an advance was ordered along the whole line. After a brief but severe struggle, Wörth was carried by General von Kirchback, and two attempts to retake it were repulsed. Meanwhile the Eleventh Corps, advancing against the French right, drove them back from Mörsbrunn to Elsasshausen, and joined hands with the centre, now moving upon Froschweiler. All along the road from Mörsbrunn they had fought a desperate hand to hand struggle, through woods and vineyards; the ground did not permit of re-forming, and the fight was man for man. The dead and wounded lay clubbed or bayonetted, French and German, side by side or locked together in the death grapple where they fell. Just outside Elsasshausen General von Bose, who commanded the corps, was severely wounded, but still managed to keep his seat in the saddle; an hour later he received a second wound at Froschweiler. Thus the French right, still fighting with unremitted courage, was forced to yield step by step along the whole position, and the progress of the German left was the signal for a concentrated attack on Froschweiler. About three o'clock in the afternoon the batteries opened fire upon it from three sides, and as the flames of the burning houses marked the havoc which the shells had made, the combined right and centre advanced to storm the heights. The Crown Prince, when he had issued his final orders, leapt upon his horse and rode after the storming columns, through Wörth and across the field of battle. At four o'clock Marshal MacMahon recognized that his position was no longer tenable, and gave orders to retire. It was at this point, in order to cover his retreat on Reichshofen, and stay the pursuit of the victorious Germans left from Elsasshausen, that he ordered that desperate charge of the brigade of Cuirassiers, which, executed with the unfaltering devotion of a forlorn hope, became one of the most tragic and heroic episodes in a story abounding in tragedy and heroism. If the roads beyond Reichshofen to Bitsch, Zabern, and Strasburg were secured, it was at a frightful cost. The French cavalry charged into a valley of death; mown down by the simultaneous fire of artillery and infantry, they lay in ordered ranks, with their faces to

H

the foe that few of them ever reached, a grisly army of the dead.

The French had fought with the utmost gallantry, and all that mortal men could do to avert disaster had been done ; but attacked simultaneously on the North, East, and South, with his retreat threatened, the Marshal had no choice but to retire.   He reached Zabern on the following day, and withdrew thence to Chalons, while other portions of the army fell back on Bitsch and Strasburg.   In the evening the Crown Prince rode over the battlefield and congratulated his troops on this decisive victory ; the massed bands were playing the national hymn as he rode up the heights of Froschweiler, greeted by the joyful cheers of officers and men.   But it was a scene of desolation that met his eyes, the dead of Reichshofen lay in grim and ghastly heaps, and there were terrible gaps in his own regiments.   On the French side some 200 officers and 9,000 men were prisoners, while the losses in killed and wounded amounted to upwards of 6,000, but the victory was obtained at the cost of 500 officers and more than 10,000 men *hors de combat*.   Amongst the distinguished French

officers who had been wounded, the Crown
Prince found General Raoult, who succumbed
to his injuries a few weeks later, lying on his
camp-bed, and, grasping his hand, spoke a few
words of kindly solicitude, and while offering
to convey any communication he might wish to
his family, desired him to command his services.

The following day, the 7th, was devoted to
rest. In the morning the Crown Prince again
rode over the field of battle, and was then for
the first time able to appreciate the full
measure of the carnage and desolation that the
day's work had made. In the garden of a
farm-house which had not suffered from the
passing storm, he found a Bavarian trooper,
who had made himself very much at home,
enjoying a quiet breakfast, and as was his wont
addressed a few friendly words to him. Standing at attention with his hand at the salute,
the honest Bavarian allowed his enthusiasm to
carry him away, and exclaimed: "If only we
had had your Royal Highness to lead us in
1866, you would have seen how we would have
thrashed those cursed Prussians!"—"I never,"
said the Crown Prince, "received a compliment
that pleased me better."

The road now lay open into the heart of France, and the advance was continued through the passes of the Vosges. The Baden contingent was told off to invest the fortress of Strasburg, and on the 11th, from head-quarters at Petersbach, the following proclamation was issued to the victorious troops :—

"SOLDIERS OF THE THIRD ARMY,

"Having with the victorious battle of Weissenburg crossed the frontier into French territory, and then by the brilliant victory of Wörth driven the French out of Alsace, we have by now advanced across the Vosges far into France, and have established communications with the First and Second Armies, before whose successful arms the foe has equally been compelled to retire.* It is your great gallantry, your high spirit, your endurance under every difficulty and exertion, that we have to thank for these important achievements. In the name of the King of Prussia, our Commander-in-Chief, and in the name of the Allied Princes, I thank you, and I am proud to find myself at the head of an army against which the enemy has hitherto been unable to hold his ground, whose deeds our common German Fatherland is watching with enthusiasm—FREDERICK WILLIAM."

* Spicheren and Saarbrück.

Simple words and unadorned, but words which went home to every man among them, who knew that appeal to their common nationality was no empty phrase with their leader, whom they would have followed, Bavarians, Würtembergers, and all of them, to the end of the world. For by now their confidence in him was equal to their regard, and each individual felt himself to be the object of his leader's forethought and solicitude. "In the hospitals," says one of his biographers, "the wounded seem to forget their pain when he drew near, and many in their delirium could speak of nothing but their leader." And how he had won the hearts of his army the following extract from the letter of a Bavarian officer will serve to illustrate :—

"It is the Crown Prince, in the first place, that we have to thank for the brotherly relations which subsist between the troops, for Prussians and Bavarians going arm-in-arm. Even the private soldiers are made his comrades for life and death : he speaks to them, not condescendingly, but with such an unmistakable ring of personal interest, and with such a genial manner, that the fellows' hearts go out to him every time. And so does his to them. So overcome was he the other day

in conferring an exceptional military distinction on a
private soldier, that in his enthusiasm he placed his
hands upon the hero's shoulders and kissed him. There
was a moment's breathless silence, and the muskets
trembled in the soldiers' hands."

On the 16th of August the Crown Prince
arrived with his Staff at Nancy, and awaited
news of the movements of the First and Second
Armies. On the 19th two officers who had
been despatched to the King's head-quarters at
Pont-à-Mousson returned with news of the three
battles that had been fought round Metz, of
the last of which, Gravelotte, they had themselves been eye-witnesses. The army of Marshal
Bazaine was now shut up in Metz, and surrounded by seven army corps under the
command of Prince Frederick Charles, it was
precluded from taking any further active part
in the campaign. On the 20th the Crown
Prince went to Pont-à-Mousson, and saw the
King for the first time after an eventful month.
The coveted distinction of the Iron Cross of
the first class was here bestowed upon him, but
with his instinctive chivalry, he declared he
could not wear it unless a similar decoration
were bestowed on General von Blumenthal.

Meanwhile the enemy was straining every nerve to form a new army at Chalons, where the broken columns of MacMahon's force had halted in their retreat. These were reinforced by the corps of General Failly and two divisions from Belfort, while large numbers of the Garde Mobile were despatched in haste from Paris. The position was well selected, but no preparations had been made for the reception of such a number of troops, and it became untenable before the rapid advance of the Germans, The day after the battle of Gravelotte a council of war had been held at the German head-quarters, at which it had been decided to form a Fourth Army (the Army of the Meuse) composed of three corps drawn off from the Second Army, to be placed under the command of the Crown Prince of Saxony. This army was to co-operate with the Third Army, and their first object was to be the destruction of the force now mustering at Chalons. On the night of the 20th, the Crown Prince rejoined his Staff at Vaucouleurs, to which the head-quarters had been moved from Nancy. In illustration of the spirit in which he carried out the instructions of his King and Father to wage no war on

the peaceful inhabitants of France, the following proclamation, issued to the inhabitants of
Nancy, will be read with interest :—

"Germany is at war with the Emperor of the
French, not with the French people. The population
need fear no hostile measures. I am occupied in
restoring the people, and especially for the town of
Nancy, the means of communication which were broken
by the French Army. I trust that business and trade
will revive, and that the authorities will remain at
their posts. I claim for the maintenance of my army
only the excess of provision which is not required for
the support of the native population. All that are
peacefully inclined, and particularly the population of
the town of Nancy, may count upon the most indulgent
treatment."

And this was literally carried out. The
military field-post was made available for the
inhabitants of Nancy, and with extraordinary
rapidity the telegraph wires and railway lines
which the French troops had destroyed were
set in working order again.

The fortress of Toul, which lay on the line of
march, offered a determined resistance. The
Crown Prince had ordered that the town was
to be spared as much as the exigencies of war

would permit, and especially that the Cathedral, a masterpiece of Gothic architecture, was to be kept well out of the line of fire. Bombarded for a whole day, Toul still held out, and the troops investing the fortress were ordered to rejoin the main body marching on Chalons, a detachment being left behind to mask it until the reserves came up, when the surrender was to be enforced. On the 23rd head-quarters were at Ligny. The King had left Pont-à-Mousson that morning, and after passing the night at Commercy, was timed to arrive at Ligny towards noon on the 24th. The streets of the little town were bright with uniforms, and all its inhabitants had crowded out to see the young commander of the Third Army, who, surrounded by his Staff, was awaiting the King's arrival. As the clock struck twelve a Hussar came galloping across the market-place and delivered a sealed order to the Prince, who hastily read its contents, and passed it on to General Blumenthal. There was great news. The French had evacuated Chalons on the 21st, and the town was already occupied by the German cavalry. The King arrived soon after one o'clock at Ligny, and the changed aspect of

affairs was considered. The direction north-
wards taken by Marshal MacMahon's Army
afforded strong grounds for the presumption
that it was the Emperor's intention, if possible,
to relieve Bazaine, and intercepted despatches
subsequently confirmed the accuracy of this
surmise. His first plan, to retire on Paris with
the army of Chalons, was abandoned in defer-
ence to reports from the capital, where the
Empress Eugenie warned him that to abandon
Bazaine and to return himself to Paris would
be the signal for revolution.

In the King's head-quarters at Bar-le-Duc a
council of war was held. The determination to
despatch the Fourth Army and the two Bavarian corps only of the Third Army, to intercept
Marshal MacMahon's progress, was combated
by the Crown Prince, who maintained that it
was of paramount importance that all available
forces should combine to strike a decisive blow
in the North, even if the advance on Paris were
delayed. His advice, supported by the weight
of General Blumenthal's opinion, prevailed, and
consequently the whole of the Third Army, in
conjunction with the Fourth, faced round to
the right and hurried by forced marches to the

North.   On the 28th reconnaissances took place
which left no further doubt as to the where-
abouts of Marshal MacMahon's Army.   After
a series of engagements in which the Crown
Prince of Saxony carried off the palm at Beau-
mont, the French drew back on the fortress of
Sedan, which, on the evening of the 31st August,
was surrounded on three sides by the German
troops.

It would be out of the question here, in the
short space which can be accorded to it, to give
any account of the memorable battle which
dealt the French Empire its death-blow.
Fighting began at daybreak ; Marshal Mac-
Mahon had drawn up his army in a semi-circle
round Sedan, extending from the north by
east to south ; the west was undefended, and
passage over the Meuse at Donchéry was thus
open to the German advance.   The task before
the Third and Fourth Armies, which the two
Crown Princes led, under the supreme command of the King himself, was to surround the
French position, preventing the possibility of
an eastward move, and at the same time
cutting off their retreat across the Belgian
frontier to the north, while, to meet the

eventuality of a westward movement, should the three sides of their front be driven back, the Sixth Army Corps had been detached to take up a strong position some twenty miles to the west of Sedan, with instructions to hold the roads and passes till the main body had time to come up. By four o'clock in the afternoon the French positions were all in the hands of the Germans, and a living wall, consisting of eight Army Corps, surrounded the whole French army in the fortress of Sedan. A brief pause ensued; only to the north the cannon thundered, and in the village of Bazeilles a desperate fight still raged in the ruined streets. Then, as no message of surrender came, the guns began to play on the devoted fortress, great clouds of smoke rolled up, and forked flames began to issue from the burning houses.

Colonel von Bronsart, who was despatched by the King to demand the surrender, found a white flag raised upon the walls, and was admitted within the gates. He had asked to be led to the General in command, and was conducted to a room in the Prefecture, where he found himself face to face with the Emperor

Napoleon. From him the Emperor learned that the King of Prussia was present with the besieging army, and despatched General Reille in company with Colonel von Bronsart to deliver to his Majesty the celebrated letter, in which he wrote that, having failed to find death in the midst of his troops, there was nothing left him but to surrender his sword. Shortly before their arrival the King and the Crown Prince had met. It was now seven o'clock. We are all familiar with that twilight picture ; the veteran King standing on a slight eminence, close behind him the Crown Prince, Bismarck, Moltke, Blumenthal ; General Reille advancing towards them with bare head, and the fateful letter in his hand. Three years before General Reille had been in attendance on the Crown Prince during his visit to the French Exhibition. The latter recognizes him, and immediately steps forward to greet him. The King reads the letter, and passes it to the Princes who are with him, and to his Staff, then he turns to the Crown Prince and clasps him to his heart. It had not been known from the first that the Emperor was himself in Sedan ; with his surrender there was at least a hope that the war which had already entailed such heavy sacrifices was at an end.

But the end was not yet to be. MacMahon's army were all prisoners of war, the army of Bazaine was interned at Metz : but the events of the 4th of September in Paris decided an advance on the capital. On the 6th, the King and Crown Prince arrived in Rheims, and a few days were devoted to rest. The people of Rheims were astonished to see the Commander of the Third Army, accompanied only by one or two of his Staff, quietly walking through the streets of their city, and studying the marvels of their famous Cathedral. Every measure of indulgence was accorded to the population during the German occupation ; an order from head-quarters gave instructions that no troops were to be quartered on the poorer inhabitants, and the local newspapers bore witness to the courtesy and moderation of their invaders. During his stay at Rheims, the Crown Prince addressed an appeal to all the States of Germany, to join in founding an institution similar to that which he had inaugurated in 1864 for the relief of the victims of war. " As this war," he wrote, " has called out an united

German Army, in which the sons of every race
are contending in brotherly rivalry for the palm
of valour, so let the provision for the invalided
and the destitute whom war will leave on our
hands be an undertaking which the whole
German race shall co-operate in."

Meanwhile, at home in Germany, the women's
work was no less zealous than that of their sons
and husbands at the front.   The Queen and
the Crown Princess were incessantly at work,
organizing help for the destitute at home, and
relief for the wounded and the prisoners.
Near the French frontier almost every house
had been turned into a hospital.   The
Crown Princess herself was established at
Hamburg, in order to be nearer to the seat
of war, and in the great " Lazareth "* here,
under her direct superintendance, as many
as a thousand beds were at one time made
up.   The Crown Princess's work was addition-
ally arduous, as she had to pay frequent visits
to her sister, Princess Alice, at Darmstadt,
whose baby was born in October while her
husband was away at the war.   Yet hardly

* A full account of this institution has been published by
Miss Florence Lees (Mrs. Craven).

a day passed without her attendance, not a patient lay there who did not receive some kindly word of sympathy, a sympathy that went directly home to each of those who knew that their royal leader had never spared himself in battle, and that there were no less anxious hearts in the old Hamburg Palace than in the humblest cottage that had sent a father or a son to fight.

At his head-quarters of Coulommiers, on the 15th September, the Crown Prince occupied the house in which King Frederick William III., with his three eldest sons, had rested, during the advance of the Allies to Paris in 1814. On the 19th the soldiers of the Third Army looked down upon the distant spires and domes of Paris, and on the following day the Crown Prince established himself in the Prefecture at Versailles. On the arrival of the King he gave up this residence to his father, and transferred his own head-quarters to the villa " Les Ombrages," the property of Madame Andrée Walther. And so the long siege began with its repeated sorties and all its well-known incidents. The news of the fall of Metz was received at Versailles on the 28th October, and the King commemorated this event by creating a new precedent in the family of Hohenzollern, in bestowing the bâton of Field-Marshal on his son and his nephew, Prince Frederick Charles. At the close of the rescript in which he announced this determination to his son, after commenting on the brilliant achievements of the Third Army, he said: "You are, therefore, entitled to the highest grade of military rank, and I hereby appoint you Field-Marshal. It is the first time that this distinction, which I also confer upon Frederick Charles, has been granted to Princes of our house. But the successes gained in this campaign have been of a character, and have led to issues of an importance, entirely without a precedent hitherto, and, therefore, I feel justified in departing from the tradition of our family. What I as a father feel, in being able to express to you my own thanks, and the country's, in such a form as this, it needs no words to describe. Your loving and grateful father, WILLIAM."

And so Christmas came, the first Christmas

I

from home. The bitter Winter weather had
set in with terrible severity ; but there was
not wanting the brighter side. The French
population of Versailles had found a friend
in their enemy, a friend whose ears were
always open to listen to an honest grief,
who had guaranteed their town and its
treasures his royal protection, and who did
all that lay in his power to alleviate the
horrors of war, so that even here the " Notre
Fritz " was fast becoming a household word.
When the guns of Mont Valérien opened fire
on St. Cloud, it was the German troops under
his command who saved all that was saved
from the treasures of the Palace, the removable
works of art and the library ; and, on the appeal
of M. Régnault, the distinguished scientist, he
organized a little expedition to save all that
was irreplaceable, the models, the drawings,
and the moulds, from the China factory of
Sèvres, which was also in danger of destruction from the French fires. " *Fas est et ab
hoste doceri.*" The subjoined letter, from his
hostess in Versailles to a friend, which has
recently been published in Germany, speaks for
itself :—

" Those were indeed bad times, but we thought ourselves happy to be under the protection of that stately
and friendly gentleman, who appears to us, as we now
think of him, to have been a good genius who warded
off mischief from our household. Although, according
to the laws of war, he was our master, and the owner
for the time of all that we had, he behaved himself
always as if he were our guest. I can never forget the
gentleness with which he used to ask for anything,
whether for himself or his Adjutant, apologizing for
giving us trouble, fearful of causing any inconvenience,
and enquiring whether this or that would interfere with
our own arrangements. On Christmas Eve, when a huge
chest arrived from Berlin for the Crown Prince, he
invited his hostess and her family to partake of his
Christmas cake. 'This cake,' said he, as he cut off
slices for the French ladies, ' was baked by my wife,
and you must oblige me to taste it.' He then chatted to
them about the Christmas festival in his own happy
household, and translated passages from the letter of the
Crown Princess and the letters of his two eldest
children." " In those fateful days," she continues,
" we learned to know the whole good and open heart of
your late Emperor. On the terrible 19th of January,
1871, when there was fighting at Mount Valérien,
Bougival, and St. Cloud, and our troops were driven
back upon Paris, many thousands of my fellow-country-
men were taken prisoners. At six o'clock in the
evening the Crown Prince had learned that among

them there were several men who were not professional
soldiers — lawyers, artists, teachers, merchants, and
others.   He asked the French officers who were taken
prisoners to notify to these civilians that if they gave
their names to him he would place escorts at their
service, so that they might return to their homes and
work.   This generous *noblesse* in your Prince made a
deep impression upon the French mind.   It has never
been forgotten, and I know with what profound respect
the knightly conqueror was spoken of at the time.   The
older folk in France, in whom the recollection of those
days must always abide, hold the memory of the noble
Emperor Friedrich in the greatest esteem."

Just after Christmas the heavy siege guns,
which had at length arrived, opened fire on
the city and its surrounding forts.   The Crown
Prince himself was at first against the bom-
bardment, but the terrible losses of the
German troops in the bloody battle before
Paris, and the unprecedented severity of
the Winter, made it imperative that the protracted seige should be terminated as soon as
possible.

Meanwhile the long-desired consummation of
the German ideal was drawing near.   After the
battle of Sedan, the South German States had
signified their readiness to adhere to the

Northern Confederation ; before Christmas all preliminaries were complete, and the Princes, on the proposition of the King of Bavaria, joined with the Northern Diet in inviting King William to assume the Imperial Dignity over an united Germany. The 18th of January, 1871, was fixed for the solemnization of this great event, and the Crown Prince was entrusted with all the preparations for the ceremony. Every regiment in the army of investment was instructed to send its colours in charge of an officer and two non-commissioned officers to Versailles, and all the higher officers who could be spared from duty were ordered to attend, for the army was to represent the German nation at this memorable scene. The Crown Prince escorted his father from the Prefecture to the palace of Versailles, where all the German Princes or their representatives were assembled in the Galerie des Glaces. A special service was read by the military chaplains, and then the Emperor, mounting on the dais, announced his assumption of Imperial authority, and instructed his Chancellor to read the Proclamation issued to the whole German nation. Then the Crown Prince, as the first subject of the Empire, came forward, and performed the solemn act of homage, kneeling down before his Imperial Father. The Emperor raised him and clasped to his arms the son who had toiled and fought and borne so great a share in achieving what many generations had desired in vain, and fulfilling the prophetic words of King Frederick William IV. : "An imperial crown must be won upon the field of battle."

The following day the last desperate sortie from the beleagured city took place. The battle was in the immediate vicinity of Versailles, and the Crown Prince was on the field throughout the day. The French fought with the courage of despair, for the city was exhausted, and unless they could dislodge the Germans from their positions and break through, surrender was inevitable. But when the early darkness closed, this final effort had not availed, and four days afterwards the first overtures were made for a cessation of hostilities.

On the 7th of March the Crown Prince left Versailles. The war was over, and on the last Sunday, as he sat at service in the little church, which he had never failed to attend during his long residence there, the words of the text, "How beautiful upon the mountains are the feet of him that bringeth good tidings, that publisheth peace," must have fallen upon his ears with a peculiar sweetness and a deeper meaning than ever before. After a brief journey to Rouen and Amiens, to inspect the Army of the North, and convey the Emperor's thanks to General von Goeben for his decisive victory at St. Quentin, he rejoined his Imperial Father at Nancy, where he issued his last address to his army. "I take my leave of you," it concluded, "Prussian and Bavarian corps, soldiers of Würtemberg and Baden, with the hope and in full confidence that the brotherhood of arms and the spirit of union cemented on the bloody field of battle may never disappear, but increase in vitality and strength, to the honour, the glory, and the blessing of our common Fatherland." But the parting was not to be a final one, for, needless to say, he was at Munich in July, when the Bavarian troops returned to make their triumphal entry. It was a touching meeting, and the words which he spoke at

the ensuing banquet were a message to every
man who had fought under his command,
which he might bear back with pride to his
mountain village, and repeat in time to come
with all those memories and episodes which
many a cottage home throughout the length
and breadth of Germany still teems with. " In
this campaign," he said, " I learned what we
may expect from Bavaria in good and evil days.
With the help of the Bavarians we have won
an honourable peace, which we hope will
endure. And as in war they did their duty,
so may they now emulate the rest of the
German family in furthering the arts of
peace, and in practising in peace the virtues
of a soldier."

After the war of 1870, it became the Crown
Prince's annual duty to inspect the military
contingents of the South German States, and
the associations of the great campaign were
thus continually refreshed. It was ever his
aim to bind faster those bonds of union which
his personal influence had done so much to promote, and, by guaranteeing to the various
component elements of the Empire respect for
their individual character and institutions, to

enlist the public sympathy for the changed order of things.

From Nancy it was one long triumphal progress home. Berlin was reached on the 17th of March ; and, though no official reception was allowed, the Royal carriage in which the King and the Crown Prince were to be seen side by side could only proceed at a foot pace through the dense masses that crowded the streets, cheering them with the cheers of a triumphant nation. With one pretty picture the record of the great campaign may fitly close, when, a little later, in response to the call of the people who thronged about his Berlin Palace, a window opened, and they saw in the midst of his young family, and beside the Crown Princess, the hero of so many victories, happy in his own home, with his youngest child in his arms.

Men have judged and will judge his military genius differently. How thorough was his practical knowledge of the soldier's business is clear from the fact that the new drill regulations for the infantry, which by order of the reigning Emperor are to supersede the old ones, had been long planned by him. It was his decisive march at Königgrätz which decided the fate of the day, it was his insistence on the necessity of leading the whole of his Army to Sedan that ensured the surrender of Marshal MacMahon's Army and the person of the Emperor Napoleon. Few great leaders can show such an unvarying record of successes, and none have possessed in a higher degree the most indispensable quality of the successful soldier, the power of attaching to himself the love and confidence of his followers. He showed a rare and striking example of simplicity and unselfishness to his soldiers. He never admitted luxuries, and would not even accept necessaries if he knew that his men were without food and drink. His thought was always for others, never for himself. The verdict of an Englishman, who had the most exceptional opportunities of observing the events which have just been described, cannot fail to be interesting to English readers. General Sir Beauchamp Walker, who in his capacity as British Military Attaché, and no less as a personal friend, accompanied the Crown Prince's Staff through the campaigns of 1866 and 1870, writes :—

" The great characteristic which distinguished him
was his coolness in difficulty; whatever happened, he
and Blumenthal kept their heads clear.   His judgment
was calm in action, his consideration was humane in
success.   What more can one say of the noblest man I
have ever known ? "

VI.

1871—1887.

VI.

1871—1887.

HITHERTO we have followed in the Prince's footsteps, along the path of public duty, and through scenes of continual activity. Now, a long period of peace lies before us, and while considering this quieter picture, we may also glance back again and see how the intervals of rest were spent, and what were the interests and occupations of one who, though circumstances had made him a soldier, was at heart a man of peace. A love of study, an enthusiasm for Art, with a full consciousness of its lofty and ennobling mission, continued with him throughout his life, while he found in the Crown Princess one who shared his cultivated tastes, and actively co-operated in directing those labours of love which it became his especial mission to promote. His own words will best testify what he held the aim of all true Art to be. Speaking at the opening of the Jubilee

Exhibition of the Berlin Academy, in 1886, he said : " But look to it, that our Art be never untrue to its high calling, to be for mankind, high and low, rich and poor, that elevating and spiritualizing influence which helps man up to God. -- Then, after that, let it fulfil its other calling—the union of nations and individuals, with all their different utterances, in the common worship of the ideal."

Needless to say, their Court at Berlin was a meeting place for all that was remarkable in various fields of culture. In Berlin and Vienna, of all the European capitals, the distinctions of class are still most rigorously marked, and there is accordingly less social intercourse between the various grades and faculties. Moreover, party spirit still runs very high, opinions coincide with social positions, and the mutual antipathy of the various political denominations is by no means confined to the precincts of the Chamber. The parties at the Crown Prince's Palace, however, formed a bright exception to this somewhat monotonous uniformity of clannishness, and there would be gathered together scholars and theologians, archæologists and explorers, artists and men of letters, without distinction of birth or political opinion. Many a young and unknown singer, and many a struggling musician, have owed their first introduction to the public notice to the Winter concerts at their palace, and all that was new in the field of design, all that was original or remarkable in Art, was assured beforehand of their interest and support. Our own countrymen can bear witness to the fact that no English author or painter of eminence whom business or pleasure took to Berlin, ever failed to find a warm welcome there; and it was always matter for regret if any such passed through the capital unnoticed or unknown.

It was therefore a peculiar satisfaction to the Crown Prince, debarred as he was by the rule he had made himself, from any participation in affairs of State, when the office of Protector of Public Museums was conferred upon him. Those who have seen them before his interest and energies were enlisted in their behalf, and since, have testified to the extraordinary development and improvement of these collections under his sympathetic control. The Old Museum, founded but little more than fifty

K

years ago, has few rivals in Europe in com-
pleteness, certainly none in arrangement. The
pictures, judiciously added to by recent pur-
chases, for the most part from England,
though still comparatively few in number, are
thoroughly representative of the various schools
in their rise and evolution ;—the print room,
enriched under the Prince's *regimé* by the
famous acquisitions from the Hamilton Collec-
tion, is probably the best managed institution
of its kind that exists ;—the marbles from
Pergamos, recovered by the indomitable perse-
verance of Herr Humann, have under his
auspices been added to reinforce the weaker
side of the Museum, its classical sculpture ;
while it can show, what we in England, with
all our wealth of treasures, have not yet been
able to afford ourselves, a gallery of casts from
the great sculptures of the world, which it was
his aim to render complete. The Museum of
Industrial Art, corresponding to our own
Museum at South Kensington, has grown up
entirely under the supervision of the Crown
Prince and Princess. A third institution, the
Ethnological Museum, in which he took the
keenest interest, is still in process of arrange-

ment, and though already open, will not be completed for some time to come.*

But it was not only the moral and intellectual progress of the people which the Prince and Princess have been ever zealous to promote; the material prosperity was a matter of no less concern. And so well was their devotion to this work understood in Germany that, on the celebration of their silver wedding, the present which the country placed in their hands

---

* In an eloquent and touching speech, at a meeting held on the 1st of July, Dr. Richard Schöne, the Director-General of the Royal Berlin Museums, summed up the great services rendered to Art by the departed Emperor. He enumerated the new Museums that had been inaugurated under his fostering hand, and described the efforts made by him to place the collections at Berlin on a footing of equality with those of other countries. The excavations at Olympia, he added, would remain a permanent monument of his zeal for, and devotion to, knowledge. "In the midst of a whole nation's mourning," he said, "they may scarcely venture to raise their voices, whose privilege it was to serve and to labour under him, in that more restricted field to which the Emperor Frederick, as Crown Prince, on behalf of his Imperial father, bestowed his special protection. But if, as long as the light of his eyes was not darkened, our mouths were closed in respectful reserve, now, at least, that he has gone from us, we may be permitted, over his grave, to give full expression to the reverence, the love, and the unalterable gratitude, which we had learned to feel for him."

was a sum £50,000, collected from the highest
and the lowest, and in every portion of the
Empire, to be distributed as they judged fit,
among the various charities with which they
were connected. How thoroughly this gift
was appreciated appears from their message of
thanks : " We must express our especial satisfaction at the fact, that our silver wedding has
been made the occasion of giving to the day
on which we made our marriage vow, and
founded, with God's help, the happiness of our
lives, its fairest consecration, and a significance
which our feelings and our aspirations approve,
by the inauguration of charitable institutions,
and by collections for objects at once noble and
of public utility."

Space would fail to enumerate all the founda-
tions and institutions which owe their existence
to the initiative of the royal pair, or in which
they have taken an active interest. The so-
called " Workmen's Colonies," whose object is
the reclaiming of tramps and finding temporary
occupation for the unemployed ; the " Fort-
bildung's Schule" institutions for the technical
and practical education of working-men in their
leisure hours, owe much to the Crown Prince's

promotion and patronage ; while it needs but
to mention the Society for the Promotion of
Health in the Home, the Victoria School for
the Training of Nurses, the Victoria Foundation
for the Training of Young Girls in Domestic
and Industrial Work, to show the practical
nature of the public services to which they
devoted themselves with the cordial co-operation of the municipal officers of Berlin.   Broad
and tolerant in religious opinion, the Crown
Prince was a determined opponent of the anti-
Semitic movement, and a firm supporter of the
liberty of conscience.   He was a zealous
protector of the order of Freemasons, and a
number of speeches made by him to various
lodges are on record, in which the same key-
note is always struck, the practical work they
have to do, and the necessity of obsolete
customs and traditions yielding to the law of
human progress.

But it was especially at Potsdam, in the
Summer months, away from the restraints
of the capital and the absorbing calls of social
and public duties, that the home-life of the
Soldier-Prince displayed its brightest side.
The occupations afforded by the little farm

at Bornstedt, the visits to the schools, the
care of poorer and humbler neighbours, have
been already alluded to. A charming picture
was afforded every year, as Christmas came
round, when all the tenants of the Bornstedt
estate and their children met round the
Christmas-tree and the long tables ranged
with presents, to distribute which the
kindly landlord and his family never
failed to come from Berlin. And again,
in the Summer, when the school-feast came
round, and the playing ground of the little
Princes and Princesses was filled with tiny
beings, shy and full of awe at first, but
before long brimming over with excitement
and delight, and carrying away a memory
which would never be forgotten of those
who led their romps, and stood by to watch
their merry games. Indeed, the Crown
Prince and Princess were never happier
than when they were surrounded by the
children of the poor; and every school or
institution with which they were in any way
connected was sure of its annual invitation.

The education of their own children had
from the first absorbed their anxious care.

The young Princes were brought up in the strictest simplicity, and early encouraged to take their part in those offices of kindness and charity in which their parents found a pleasurable duty, while by frequent association with their humbler brethren they were taught to understand the harder realities of life. The Crown Prince himself had been the first of his house to enter a public university. In the case of his two sons, a more striking departure from ancient usage was decided upon, and when Prince William was fifteen years of age, and Prince Henry twelve, they were sent to the Gymnasium at Cassel, which occupies the place in Germany of one of our greater public schools. They were left by their parents, who accompanied them thither, in charge of General von Gottberg, their military governor, and Dr. Hinzpeter, their former tutor. Prince William, who was placed at once in one of the higher forms, passed his final examinations after some two years' study, and when he came of age in 1877, on completing his 18th year, quitted Cassel to join the regiment in which his father had also begun his military career, nearly thirty years before. Prince Henry, who was destined for a naval career, on leaving Cassel, joined the cadet ship "Niobe," at Kiel, and after a year's apprenticeship, started in the "Prince Adalbert" for a two year's cruise round the world. The two young Princes inherited from their mother their taste for English games and field sports. The first lawn-tennis court in Berlin and Potsdam, where the game is now growing popular, was, needless to say, in the gardens of the New Palace ; the river Havel, with its wooded lakes, was near for bathing and boating ; and on a little model frigate presented by our King William IV. to the King of Prussia, they learned their first essays in navigation. There is no one who follows with a keener interest all great events in the world of sport and athletics in England than the present German Emperor.

The youngest daughter of the Crown Prince and Princess was born on the 22nd of April, 1872, and named Margaret, after her god-mother, the reigning Queen of Italy, who came to Potsdam for the christening ceremonies. The close friendship of the heirs to the thrones

of Germany and Italy was bearing fruit, for
in the following year (1873) King Victor
Emmanuel, who until the downfall of the
French Empire had from a sense of obligation
maintained sympathetic relations with the
Emperor Napoleon, paid a visit to the Court
of Berlin, which was returned by the Crown
Prince immediately, and by the Emperor himself as soon as public duty admitted of his
absenting himself from the capital.   Latterly
there were few years when business or pleasure
did not take the Crown Prince over the Alps.
Many will remember, with special interest at
the present time, an incident which occurred
during his visit to Rome in 1878, when he
went as the Emperor's representative to attend
the funeral of the founder of the new Italian
kingdom.   Appearing on the balcony of the
Quirinal with King Humbert and Queen Mar-
gherita, he lifted the little Prince of Naples in
his arms to show him to the people.   The
quick imagination of the Roman crowd seized
on the symbolic side of this natural movement,
and gave vent to the most enthusiastic demonstrations of delight.

    In the same year, after the marriage of his

eldest daughter, Princess Charlotte, with the
Hereditary Prince of Saxe-Meiningen, the
Crown Prince had accompanied the Crown
Princess to England. During their visit to
Hatfield House in the beginning of June came
the news of the desperate attempt of the
socialist Nobiling on the life of the Emperor
William. The evening after the receipt of
this alarming news the Crown Prince and
Princess were once more in Berlin, where the
Government was placed in the Prince's hands
during the Emperor's temporary disablement.

It was not until the last month of 1878 that
the aged Monarch was sufficiently recovered to
resume the reins of government. During these
six months the Congress of Berlin had met
and separated. One famous State document,
bearing the Crown Prince's signature, belongs
to this period of the Regency, a letter to Pope
Leo XIII., at the moment when those negotia-
tions with the Vatican were re-opened, which
paved the way for an ultimate reconciliation.
The following extract contains the two essential
points : the firm determination of the Prussian
Sovereign to remain independent of the control
of the Church, and the profession of readiness

to approach the questions at issue in a conciliatory spirit :—

" The demand advanced in your letter of the 17th
of April, that the constitution and the laws of Prussia
should be modified to meet the principles of the
Roman Catholic Church, is one which no Prussian
Sovereign will be able to admit, because the independence of the Monarchy, which it is now my duty to
defend, as an inheritance received from my fathers and
an obligation owed to my country, would cease to be
absolute if the free development of its legislation were
to be subordinated to the control of another power without. Though it is therefore not in my power, and
perhaps not in that of your Holiness either, to remove
an antagonism of principles, which has for a thousand
years been more keenly felt in the history of Germany
than in that of any other country, I am nevertheless
prepared to meet the difficulties which both parties have
inherited in this conflict, in the peace-loving and conciliatory spirit which my convictions as a Christian
enjoin."

When the brief period of Regency was over
the Crown Prince resumed his quiet, unobtrusive
life once more ; but there was no work of public
utility, no historic centenary, no inauguration
of national monuments in which he did not take
his part, sometimes by the side of the Emperor,

sometimes as his representative. The Winter which followed these troublous times was indeed a sad one for the royal household—in December Princess Alice died, and in March fell the crushing blow which has been already alluded to, the death of the beloved Prince Waldemar.

The small English community of Berlin was sure of the Crown Prince's interest and protection, and the building of the English church, in the gardens of the Monbijou Palace, with the funds which were collected on the occasion of the Silver Wedding, was a source of continual occupation to the Crown Princess, who studied every detail herself with an artist's care. There is a pleasant memory of home about the little church, prettily situated in the Palace garden, and its completion was the realization of a long cherished dream. The speech made by the Crown Prince at the ceremony of laying the foundation stone will be especially interesting to English readers :—

"I feel," he said, " a peculiar pleasure in addressing those who have met together to-day to witness the laying of the foundation-stone of the first English church in this town ; for this act realizes a hope which not the

Crown Princess alone, but I also, have long cherished. The fulfilment of this hope, however, seemed very difficult, and would have remained so, but for the efforts, not only of the English congregation, but also of many friends and well-wishers both in England and here. I dwell with pleasure on the thought that the Emperor, in granting the use of this piece of Crown-land, has been actuated by the same feelings which prompted his brother and predecessor, King Frederick William IV., to appropriate one of the rooms of the Palace of Monbijou to the use of the English congregation, who had till then held their church services in a room at an hotel. I am glad that the anniversary of the Queen's birthday has been chosen for laying the foundation-stone of the English church, especially as the Queen's recent bereavement* prevents any other celebration of the day this year. The Prince of Wales and the other members of the Royal Family are certainly present with us in spirit to-day, for to their zealous efforts is chiefly owing the success of the *fête* in London which provided so large a portion of the funds for the building and carrying out of the plans, furnished by the talent of the eminent Berlin architect, Professor Raschdorff.

"The Crown Princess and I shall always take an additional interest in the church, because you know that the English residents, while providing it for their own worship, intend it at the same time to be a

* The death of the Duke of Albany.

memorial of the 25th anniversary of our wedding day. Let me conclude by expressing every good wish for the perfect success of the undertaking, and the hope that it may contribute towards making their foreign home more home-like to the English residents in Berlin."

"I am quite proud of my English," said the Crown Prince, in giving the manuscript of this speech to Mr. Teignmouth Shore, who had been most active in promoting the scheme, "I wrote it all out myself."

In this connection also may be mentioned an incident recorded by Mr. Perry at an interview in Buckingham Palace, many years after the old days at Bonn.

"After kind enquiries," Mr. Perry writes, "about my children, whose names he remembered after so many years, he took a little prayer-book from his desk, and holding it out to me, asked me if I remembered it. I did not. 'You lent me that,' he said, 'one Sunday when I came into your seat in the English church at Bonn, and I kept it, and always carry it about with me. I like your English service so much.'"

And so the years went by brightly and usefully, in spite of the ever-increasing difficulty

of the position, as the heir to the throne grew
older, witnessing in due course the marriage of
Prince William to Princess Augusta Victoria of
Schleswig-Holstein, witnessing the birth of
grandchildren, and all the lights and shadows
of home-life, varied by continual journeys as
duty called or pleasure; for the wandering
spirit acquired in youth was strong to the last.
One of these journeys calls for more than a
passing record. It was towards the close of
1883 that the Crown Prince was charged to
return on the King's behalf the visit that
King Alfonso of Spain had paid to the Prussian
capital. Circumstances had rendered it ex-
pedient that the nearer route through France
should be abandoned, and the journey made by
sea from Genoa to Valencia. The advent of
the Prince in Italy was invariably marked by
popular demonstrations of affection; and late
as the hour was when the Royal party arrived
in Genoa, the streets were thronged to receive
him, for it was still fresh in the people's memory
that the Crown Prince and Princess had
initiated an appeal to their own countrymen on
behalf of the sufferers in the recent calamity of
Ischia. After spending the night in the Royal

Palace, he embarked on the " Prince Adalbert," the vessel in which his son had sailed round the world, and arrived at Valencia, after a stormy passage, on the 22nd of November. At Madrid every form of festivity was instituted in his honour ; and at the Court Ball the veteran General von Blumenthal, who accompanied him, was forced to take part in the royal quadrille, a performance which he said weighed more heavily on him than the prospect of another campaign would have done.

All was new ground to the Crown Prince, who spent every available moment in the picture galleries, and after a fortnight at Madrid he devoted another week to a tour among the classic cities, finding a new revelation of Art in the marvels of the Alhambra, in the great Mosque, with its thousand columns of the city of the Caliphs, in the vast design of the Cathedral of Seville. During his stay at Madrid a telegram reached him from Berlin, instructing him to return by Rome, ostensibly to thank the King for his hospitality at Genoa, but also to afford an opportunity for a visit to the Pope, whose conciliatory policy promised to effect an end so ardently desired by the Emperor William, the

re-establishment of peace with the Catholic
Church and party. In Rome the Crown Prince
was the guest of the King at the Quirinal.
A visit direct from the Quirinal to the Vatican
could scarcely, in the actual state of relations,
have been acceptable. A curious compromise
was therefore resorted to. From the Quirinal the
Prince drove first to the German Embassy.
Thence he proceeded to the official residence of
the Prussian Minister accredited to the Pope,
and there, dismounting from the carriage which
bore the arms of the house of Savoy, he drove
with his Staff in the carriages of the Prussian
Legation to the Vatican. He had previously
disarmed the possibility of misinterpretation on
the part of the national party, by placing, in
the morning, a wreath on the grave of King
Victor Emmanuel. There was no other person
present at his interview with the Pope, and
what passed remained at the time subject for
conjecture. The incident is introduced here
not on account of its political aspect, but in
illustration of the admirable tact and judgment
through which the Prince succeeded in offend-
ing neither party. " Being the guest of the
King of Italy," he said himself, "I have also

L

been able to pay a visit to the Pope. These
are facts of great importance, of which our
country will reap the benefit."

The mention of Rome recalls the memory of
one who, having witnessed there the solution of
the Italian question, was during thirteen years
the Queen's representative at Berlin, and who
acquired, as few foreigners could ever hope to
do, the confidence both of the Court and the
Government. In Lord Ampthill, gifted as he
was in an extraordinary measure with social
and intellectual charm, the Crown Prince and
Princess found a warm friend, and they took
the greatest pleasure in the society both of
himself and of his wife--a friend of the Crown
Princess's early days. His little villa on the
hill near Sans Souci was a favourite spot with
them, and the scene of many cherished recol-
lections. An admirable scholar and a qualified
critic, he was at the same time a thorough man
of the world, a master of the literature of four
languages, and he possessed the gift of expression in each ; his mind was a storehouse of
memories and portraits, and while it was a
privilege to listen to his conversation, he
possessed the rare and lovable quality of

seeming to bestow his best upon whomsoever he might for the moment be in contact with. His early death, in 1884, was a great grief and a genuine loss to the royal pair, in whose lives he had become such a familiar figure. The day after his death the Crown Prince came himself to the little villa to lay a wreath upon the coffin, and he took a rosebud from it away with him to keep.

When in the summer of 1886 the University of Heidelberg celebrated its fifth centenary, the Crown Prince was again the Emperor's representative. His speech on this occasion, apart from its intrinsic merit, and its telling force in the mouth of one who was looked on as the typical representative of United Germany, has also a touching interest from the fact that it is the last important public speech which he ever made in that clear, familiar, ringing voice of his. So soon after the shadows began to close around him, and the silence fell. This speech, which inevitably loses much in translation, is so remarkable that it shall be given unabridged. Addressing himself to the Grand Duke of Baden as Chancellor, and the assembled University, he said :—

"As bearer of the greetings and congratulations of
His Majesty the Emperor, I am filled with pride and
pleasure at the enthusiasm with which on these festal
days her sons, both young and old, have gathered round
their princely Chancellor, looking back with him on the
glorious history of this University, and realizing, with
gratitude to God, that in the 500 years of her existence
she has never known a brighter period than that in
which we live. Founded in the dawn of our age of
culture, the University of Heidelberg has experienced
and shared in all the changeful phases through which
the German character has passed, in the hard-won
development of its individuality. She has flourished
and drooped in turn; suffered and battled for the
freedom of belief and research; has known sorrow
and exile, that at last, supported by the firm and
gentle hand of her royal protector, she might cover
her honourable wounds with the gala robe of
victory.

"Like the German nation, whose noblest possessions
her voice was ever raised to defend, she has seen fulfilled the desire of centuries. Her shield of honour
gleams the brighter in the sun of our united Fatherland. With deep emotion I recall to-day the
momentous hour* in which your Royal Highness was

* At the ceremony at Versailles, when the Emperor
assumed the Imperial dignity, the Grand Duke of Baden was
the first to step forward and call for a cheer for the "German
Emperor."

the first to greet the leader of our victorious nation by
the noble name of Emperor. This recollection has for
me a deep significance at the festival which we are
celebrating. To be the first to put in action a great and
good resolve is a privilege of your illustrious house and
of this famous University.

"It is my pleasant duty in the mission I fulfil to
acknowledge to her honour how loyally Heidelberg performed her part in fostering those mental and social
conditions which were the first step to our national
regeneration. She was ever liberally hospitable to
teachers as to pupils. From every province they
flocked to her, and in the loving arms of their Alma
Mater, they realized once more that a greater mother
was their parent.

"So here in the quiet of the student's life was
developing what history, after long wanderings, has
vouchsafed us. In the south-western corner of the
Empire, near the old frontier, and therefore near the
danger, the son of the North learned to love the son of
the South as his brother, that he might return again to
his home, and spread abroad the fair faith that all the
people are one people, which faith is our treasure and
our strength.

"And now that we possess it once more, this blessing
of unity, there is blown back from the mighty whole a
breath which brings vigour to the dear old home where
we were educated. Wider grow the aims of knowledge,
wider our aspirations, more grateful the duty of the

teacher to proclaim them, and of the pupil to appreciate them.

"The Fatherland and the Academic Commonwealth can only exercise a beneficial influence on one another if they preserve the same virtues in their respective spheres of activity. The higher the results we achieve in science and in history, the loftier the aims to which we aspire, the greater prudence and self-denial we shall need.

"My dearest wishes and my confident hope, which I offer to the University to-day, are recorded in the appeal I make to teachers and to scholars, to bear in mind the duty most imperiously devolving on us, when elated with success, in learning as in living, to be conscientious and severe in intellectual discipline, and to promote the feeling of brotherhood among comrades, that from the spirit of independence and the love of peace may ensue the necessary force to develop all the forms of our national life. So may it be granted to this University, one of the oldest schools of German culture, to remain in energy her youngest."

In the Winter a severe cold brought on a hoarseness, which was not at first regarded as of serious importance, and was lightly treated by the Emperor himself, who would say with a smile, "I cannot sing," apologizing for his enforced silence. But as the weeks went by, and no improvement was revealed,

there were not a few who began to feel a
certain anxiety; and the festivities on the
22nd of March, when the Emperor William
attained his ninetieth birthday, and Prince
Henry was formally betrothed to his cousin,
Princess Irene of Hesse, when he was called
upon to represent the aged Monarch at a
number of functions, were a severe strain upon
his overtaxed energies. A cure at Ems was
recommended, but proved of no service; and
it was after his return from Ems that those
sinister rumours first began to spread abroad,
which enlisted for the royal patient not
only the sympathy of Germany, but that of
Europe and of countries far beyond the seas,
where his name had become a proverb for
all that was lovable and generous and of
good report; a sympathy which, we have
the Chancellor's guarantee for it, was the
one source of gratification and consolation
to the last dark weeks of the aged Emperor's
waning life.

He was nevertheless well enough to take
part in the rejoicings at the Queen's Jubilee,
and as he rode in the procession in the
white uniform of the Cuirassiers his stately

presence and his kindly, friendly face, together
with the sentiment of some grave crisis
hanging over the head of the soldier-hero,
made a deep and lasting impression on all
who were present at that memorable scene.
Men spoke of nothing but the German Crown
Prince, as if they, too, had a special claim
upon him. They knew that he was gifted
with all the virtues which Englishmen admire,
and that he loved our country well, and
through the dark year that followed there
was but one topic that all were absorbed
in, one prayer that went up through the
length and breadth of the land, that this
man's life might be spared. It will have a
pathetic interest to many who were witnesses
of the last great public ceremony in which
he took part to know what was passing in
his own mind as he rode past, the observed
of all observers. His quick observation
was at work, noting upon that day, as
he ever did in foreign countries, anything
which struck him as worthy of admiration,
with a view to its subsequent adaptation
in his own. After his death was found in
a little pocket-book, which he carried with

him on that day, the following entry : " The ambulance arrangements on the day of the Jubilee. The drinking-troughs for horses and dogs, and the cabmen's shelters in the streets of London."

From London the Crown Prince went alone for a brief visit to Scotland, and appeared to derive great benefit from the fresh mountain air and the vigorous life he led. During his stay at Braemar he was asked by a gentleman to do him the honour of christening a steam-launch. He gave it the name of " The White Heather," showing how his thoughts still travelled back to the memory of a day, nearly thirty years before, when in these same Scotch mountains he had plucked the sprig of white heather to give to his English bride. Rejoining the Crown Princess and his three youngest daughters, the Crown Prince went from Scotland to Toblach, in Tyrol, and later to Venice and Baveno. Finally, the Villa Zirio, at San Remo, was chosen as a Winter residence, and when he re-entered Berlin it was as German Emperor. The events of last year are still too fresh in the memory of all to need recapitulation here. We all remember too well the

changing hopes and fears, the doubts that
trembled into certainty, and left no room for
hope.   It was a gloomy New Year at Berlin ;
and when the usual season of Carnival came
round there was but little heart in the
gaiety.   Ever thoughtful of others, and
mindful how important an interest is in-
volved in the social season to large numbers
of the working-classes, the Crown Prince
had sent a message from San Remo, desiring
that all should take its usual course; but
at every meeting there was present an un-
bidden guest—the sinister rumour passing
through the throng.   February the 9th, the
day upon which the operation of tracheotomy
was performed, had been fixed for the annual
subscription ball in the Royal Opera House,
the proceeds of which are devoted to the Berlin
charities.   The house was full, as ever, but
through the dense crowd the unwelcome news
began to spread, and there was no mirth in any
of the thousand faces—not a dance was danced
that night, and all the people seemed touched
as by the sense of a personal sorrow.   A month
later anxious crowds were gathered round the
Palace in Berlin.   The Emperor was sinking

from the exhaustion of age; far from the son who had been ever at his side in the hour of danger, he fought the last great battle alone. But gently sleep fell upon him, full of years and full of honour, and without a struggle, the long laborious life was closed.

VII.

1888.

VII.

1888.

On the night of the 11th of March the Emperor
Frederick reached his capital, in a wild storm
of sleet and snow; he had borne the journey
well, and the few who witnessed his arrival
were struck by his vigorous demeanour. His
old friend and ally, King Humbert, had
travelled to Genoa to salute him as Emperor
on his way, and the last meeting between the
two Sovereigns, whose lives had had so much
in common, was a very touching one. All
along the line from the German frontier,
thousands had flocked to every railway station
in the hope of obtaining a fleeting glimpse of the
illustrious traveller, and silently but sincerely
his people welcomed him home. The Chancellor
and the Ministers of State had gone as far as
Leipzig to meet the Royal train, and transact

with the Emperor such immediate business as
required his personal direction. On his arrival,
shortly after eleven, the Emperor drove straight
to the Palace of Charlottenburg, which gives
its name to a suburb some three miles from
the city. A little later, through the white
snow-covered Linden Alley, lined by troops
with flaming torches, the body of the first
German Emperor, dressed in his military cap
and cloak, with the Order of " Merit " on his
breast, was solemnly borne from the Palace to
the Cathedral where he was to lie in State.

On the following day the Emperor Frederick
issued his proclamation to the German nation,
and a rescript addressed to the Imperial
Chancellor was simultaneously published, in
which he paid a warm tribute of esteem to his
father's faithful friend and counsellor, and set
forth the principles which were to characterize
his government. These two remarkable docu-
ments, which will be found in the Appendix,
composed entirely by the Emperor's own hand,
would alone suffice to mark his brief and tragic
reign, and their lessons will not all be lost.
At last, after the long years of waiting and
restraint, his own heart might find expres-

sion ; and now, when the power came, it was
already too late. He was not even able to
look for the last time on the father he had
loved and served so well; only from the
window of his palace he watched the funeral
procession winding past to the Mausoleum
in the garden of Charlottenburg, where
Queen Louise and King Frederick William III.
lie side by side in their marble sleep. It was a
moving scene to many a war-worn veteran, that
last farewell to the good old Emperor ; it was a
moving scene to all who had lived through the
mighty changes that his reign had witnessed ;
but what must have been in the mind of the
illustrious mourner, as he turned back from the
window into his silent chamber! He also had
meant to be his people's father ; he had prepared himself with untiring devotion to duty
for his great task, the thought of which in times
before had almost overwhelmed him till his
strong faith reconquered his misgivings of
himself : he had not neglected to make
acquaintance with people of every party, class,
and calling, so as to be in touch with the inner
life and aspirations of the nation ; he had kept
his life clean and spotless, and above all little-

M

ness and spite, to be a bright example in the
eyes of men. And now, when he came to be
crowned at last, there was nothing left him to
do but to husband what strength remained to
him for the daily routine of duties that he must
needs fulfil, to give up all the rest for ever,
bravely to surrender himself and bow to the will
of God. The service of man had been his life-
long study, and now, when the time for
realization should have come, it was only given
him to teach one lesson, but that the hardest
of all to learn and the noblest of all to teach,
the lesson of self-renouncement and unmurmur-
ing resignation. To the last his force of will
maintained him, worn and harassed as he was
by all that his disease entailed upon him, and
by the oppression of his enforced silence, he left
no portion of his daily task undone, and on the
sick-bed where others rest he still worked
bravely on. When he was well enough to
spend the afternoons in the garden of the
Palace, he would send for his horses, and watch
his favourites being exercised with a look of
wistful interest. His love for animals was
great; from his earliest youth he had made a
certain race of Italian greyhounds his particular

pets, and was always to be seen in the country followed by two or three of these delicate and graceful animals, and not a day had passed in old times, either in Berlin or Potsdam, without his visiting the stables to feed with his own hand the horses who knew his footstep and expected his daily visit.

Day after day through the Spring weeks dense crowds hung round the Charlottenburg Palace, in spite of its great distance from Berlin, for the chance of seeing that beloved face at the window, or of catching a passing glimpse of him when later, as the weather mended, a few short drives were sanctioned. If the love and care of all who surrounded him, if the sympathy and admiration of the world were any consolation to the strong mind for its forced inactivity, to the strong man for his waning strength, such consolation was not wanting; and indeed it was a theme to which he constantly recurred, the sincere feeling evinced for him in foreign countries, and what most particularly touched him, the expression this feeling found in France. This is no place to intrude upon the ministries of that closer circle that watched his sick chamber and tended his latter days with loving

M 2

and unwearying devotion, but probably never has it been granted to any single individual to find such a place as he found, by the mute appeal of his pathetic story, in the hearts of all classes and all countries.

There were three bright passages in the brief three months of his reign, with the daily record of which all are still familiar. The first was the Queen's visit to Berlin, during which he perceptibly rallied ; the second, the marriage of his sailor son, Prince Henry, to Princess Irene of Hesse, at which he was able to be present ; and the third, the move from Charlottenburg to the old home at Potsdam, to which he now gave the name of "Friedrichskron"; the palace where he was born, where he had spent the happy Summers of his married days, and where he was now all too soon to close his bright and useful life. The last crisis set in very soon after his arrival at Friedrichskron, and his state was declared to be hopeless. Brave and patient as he had been throughout his long and cruel illness, with its wearing and painful recurrent crises, bravely as he had received his death-warrant, so bravely he met his end.

The 14th of June was the birthday of
Princess Sophie. He sent for her quite early
in the morning to give her the flowers he had
ordered for her, and seemed quite cheerful and
bright, but his strength was exhausted by the
progress of the disease and his long heroic
struggle against it. To the end he had " done
out the duty," he had suffered without com-
plaining, as through life he had kept his great
shield white, and now the silent Emperor
bowed his head, and was ready, if ever man was
on earth, to meet God face to face. A little
before midday on the 15th of June, surrounded
by the whole of his family, he passed away
without a struggle.

After death, his body was by his own express
wish wrapped in his military mantle, and the
Empress placed in his arms the sword he had
worn in his various campaigns ; round his neck
she hung his Grand Cross of the Order " *Pour le
Mérite*," and on his breast she laid the wreath
of oak leaves she had given him on his return
from the war of 1870.

His coffin was placed in the church where
his sons Prince Sigismund and Prince Waldemar rest, in the gardens of Sans Souci,

awaiting the Mausoleum that is to be built to
receive it. The funeral ceremony took place
upon the day of Waterloo, a bright day between
rainy days, and never were the parks and
gardens of Friedrichskron more beautiful than
on that morning, with the fresh green of the
late season, and the birds singing in all the
trees.

In the great semi-circular garden in front of
the Palace, facing the avenue which leads to
Sans Souci, the solemn procession formed ;
under the trees surrounding it troops were
drawn up, to the left infantry. to the right
calvary, amongst which were the Life Guards
with black cuirasses : there was no crowding,
the public were excluded here ; along the
avenue more troops were drawn up waiting to
join the procession. The coffin lay in the
Jasper Hall, opening on a terrace facing the
garden, and there a preliminary service took
place. Then as the coffin was placed upon the
bier, the soft and solemn singing ceased, and
the military bands stationed round the semi-
circle began a weird and melancholy music,
chorales of the German Protestant Church,
each taking up the other, and so on down the

avenue till the sound died away in the trees.
All the while muffled drums were beating.
The procession formed; the charger he had
ridden in the war of 1870, a superb chestnut,
called Wörth, which knew him and followed
him as a dog does its master, was led behind
the bier, and the veteran Field-Marshal von
Blumenthal carried the Imperial banner.   It
was a small procession, but very solemn and
impressive.   The sun shone out on the helmets
and cuirasses, on the gardens he had loved and
cared for, on the terrace where he walked in
the Summer evenings in pleasant converse with
some favoured guest, while amid the weird
music of the military bands, and the roll of the
muffled drums, the slow procession was lost in
the green of the trees.

And now in conclusion let us glance back
over the career and character of this singularly
gifted life.   The time allotted him to reign in
was too brief and troubled for the accomplishment of any public acts that could leave a
permanent trace behind them; but the whole
tendency of his example, the note of idealism
which he supplied to temper the sterner
material virtues of the national character, his

breadth and tolerance in questions of religion, the consistent record of his simple and unselfish life, will not be soon effaced, and will some day be better understood. The genius of each nation is different, and we should do ill to judge the German by our own, or to expect that like causes would necessarily lead to like effects, but the genius of every vigorous nation is progressive, and it was his merit as a ruler to have appreciated this.

To those who never knew him, it will be impossible to convey an adequate idea of his irresistible personal charm, of the smile in his eyes, and the kindly brightness of his face, which brought a contagious light and gladness wherever he entered in. His sense of humour was keen, and like all simple characters in whom the child is only gone to sleep, he delighted in innocent amusement. While none the less, though known only to his closest intimates, there lay beneath this outward brightness the inevitable accompaniment of the idealistic nature, the "eternal note of sadness," the deep depression of the earnest thinker. All who were brought into contact with him fell immediately under the charm of his manner, which, with all its naturalness and geniality, was never wanting in dignity.   And where such acquaintance ripened into closer intimacy, experience only developed a warmer admiration.   To quote once again the words of one who had exceptional opportunities for studying his character in the most trying times, in camp and on the battlefield : " He was not only the most lovable, but the noblest man with whom I have ever associated—noble in his acts, noble in his speech, noble in his judgment of others. I never knew him say an unkind thing of anyone, man or woman, living or dead—not that his judgment of others was always favourable, but it was never expressed in other than the most kindly terms." *

Destined from his birth to rule, he schooled himself to learn submission, and to abide his time in patience. Free to command the energies of his subordinates, he was full of kindly consideration, and never suffered custom to blunt his gratitude for a service loyally performed. Though constantly engaged in the public duties of his lofty station, he still found time for all those private acts of kindliness and sympathy,

* General Sir Beauchamp Walker.   Letter to the Author.

as neighbour, as master, as friend, which earn for private persons the love and admiration of their fellows. He had acquired wide and varied learning, and his high ambition was to open a royal road to knowledge to the richest and the poorest of his subjects alike. For him the earth displayed her marvels to a loving eye, and Art not vainly revealed her treasures ; he had seen much, toiled much, enjoyed much. He was essentially a man, and there was no human interest or emotion which he could not share.

An active and industrious youth, a married life crowned with many blessings, and not-un-tempered by the sorrows man is heir to, and a public career which was rich in great results, had prepared him for a brilliant and useful future. All too early, too soon for the accomplishment of many cherished plans, after an heroic endurance of pain and disappointment, he was taken from us in the pride of his manhood and strength ; and as they bore him on that Summer morning from his happy home of thirty years, there came into the present writer's mind the words :—

> " Thou art the ruins of the noblest man
> That ever lived in the tide of times."

APPENDIX.

APPENDIX.

The Emperor Frederick's Proclamation to his People.

The Emperor's glorious life is ended.

In the dearly-loved father whom I mourn, and for whom all the members of my Royal House are with me sorrowing, Prussia's loyal people has lost a King crowned with glory, the German nation has lost the founder of its unity, the re-established Empire has lost the first German Emperor.

His exalted name will remain indissolubly connected with all the greatness of the German Fatherland, in re-creating which the persistent labour of Prussia's people and Princes has found its fairest reward.

In raising the Prussian Army with unwearying and paternal care to the height of its grave mission, King William established the sure foundation of those victories which were won

under his leadership by German arms, and
from which the national unity arose.   He thus
secured the Empire that powerful position for
which till then every German heart had longed,
but hardly dared to hope.

And what he won for his people in the fire
and sacrifice of battle it was granted him
to establish and promote, through long laborious
years of government consecrated to the work of
peace.

Resting secure on her own strength, Germany
stands respected in the councils of the nations,
and only desires to enjoy and develop what she
had won, in peace.

That this is so, we must thank the Emperor
William.   His constant fidelity to duty, his
unremitting energy, labouring only for the good
of the Fatherland, supported as he was by the
self-sacrificing devotion which the Prussian
nation has ever unwaveringly shown, and
all the German races have shared.

On me have now devolved all the rights
and duties, bound up with the throne of my
House, which I am resolved faithfully to ob-
serve so long as it may please God's will that I
shall reign.

Deeply conscious of the greatness of my task, my sole endeavour will be to carry on the work in the sense in which it was begun, to make Germany a stronghold of peace, and in harmony with the federal governments, as well as with the constitutional bodies of the Empire and of Prussia, to further the prosperity of the country.

To my loyal people, which has through the story of many centuries stood by my House in good and evil days, I place my unreserved confidence. For I am convinced that, resting on the basis of the inseparable union between Prince and people, which, independently of all changes in political life, has been the imperishable heritage of the House of Hohenzollern, my throne will ever be as sure as the prosperity of the country which I am now called upon to govern, to which I promise and vow to be a just and faithful King, in joy as well as in sorrow.

May God grant me His blessing and strength for this work, to which henceforth I dedicate my life.

FREDERICK, I.R.

BERLIN, *March* 12, 1888.

Rescript addressed to the Imperial Chancellor.

" My Dear Prince,

"At the opening of my reign I feel the necessity of addressing you, for so many years the tried first servant of my father, now resting in God. You were the faithful and courageous counsellor who gave form to the aims of his policy, and secured their successful realization.

"To you the warm thanks of myself and of my House are in duty due.

"You have, therefore, a right, before all others, to know what are the guiding principles by which my rule will be governed.

"The constitutional and legal ordinances of the Empire and of Prussia must first and foremost be consolidated in the respect of the nation and in the national life. Therefore, those shocks which repeated changes in the institutions and laws of the State entail are to be avoided as far as it is possible.

The furtherance of the duties which fall to the Imperial Government must leave those stable principles undisturbed upon which hitherto the Prussian State has securely rested.

In the Empire the constitutional rights of all the Federal Governments are to be as conscientiously observed as those of the Imperial Diet ; but from both a similar respect for the rights of the Emperor will be expected. At the same time it must be kept in view that these mutual rights are only intended to serve the promotion of the public welfare, which remains the supreme law, and that new and undoubted national requirements which may make themselves felt must be satisfied in full measure.

The most indispensable and most certain guarantee for the unimpeded furtherance of this work I hold to be the maintenance in unabated strength of the defensive forces of the nation, my well-tried army, and my growing navy, which is finding important duties to perform, now that we have acquired possessions beyond the seas. Both must continually maintain that standard of efficiency and thoroughness of organization which have

N

already established their fame, and guarantee their effective service in the future.

I am resolved to govern in the Empire and in Prussia with a conscientious observation of the the provisions of their respective constitutions. For these were established by those who have gone before me in wise appreciation of the inevitable requirements of social and political life, and the questions it presents for solution, and must be respected by each and all, that their vigour and beneficent influence may be assured.

It is my will that the principle of religious toleration, which has for years been held sacred in my family, shall continue to extend its protection to all my subjects, to whatsoever religious community and creed they may belong. Every one of them stands equally near my heart, for all of them equally in the hour of danger proved their complete devotion.

In entire accord with the views of my imperial father, I shall warmly support every movement towards furthering the economical prosperity of every class of society, reconciling their conflicting interests, and mitigating, as far as may be possible, unavoidable differences, without encouraging the anticipation that every social evil can be removed by State intervention.

I consider as intimately connected with social questions the control of the education of youth. While, on the one hand, a higher cultivation must be extended to ever-widening circles, we have at the same time to beware of the dangers of half-education, of awakening demands which the nation's economic development is unable to satisfy, of neglecting the real business of education in a one-sided effort after increase of knowledge.

Only a generation growing up on the sound principle of the fear of God, and in simplicity of morals, will possess sufficient power of resistance to counteract the dangers which the whole community incurs in a time of rapid economic development, through the example of the highly luxurious life of individuals. It is my will that no opportunity be lost in the public service of manifesting all possible opposition to the temptation to inordinate expenditure.

My unbiassed consideration is assured in advance to every proposal of financial reform, if the old Prussian principle of economy will not enable us to avoid the imposition of new burdens, and to effect an alleviation of the demands that have hitherto been made.

I consider as beneficial the measure of self-government accorded to greater and smaller communities in the State. On the other hand, I suggest for examination the point whether the right of levying taxes conferred upon these communities, which is exercised by them without sufficient regard to the burdens simultaneously imposed by the Empire and the State, may not press too heavily upon the individual.

In like manner it will have to be considered whether a reform in the direction of simplification may not be admissible in the organization of the authorities, so that by reducing the number of officials an increase might be made to their emoluments.

If we succeed in maintaining in full vigour the bases of political and social life, it will afford me especial satisfaction to assist in promoting to its perfect development the progress which Art and Science in Germany can boast in so large a measure.

For the realization of these my intentions, I

count upon the devotion you have given such constant proof of, and the support of your tried experience.

May it be granted me on these principles to lead the people of Germany and Prussia to new honours in the field of practical development, with the unanimous co-operation of all the organs of the Empire, the devotion of the people's representatives, and all the official bodies, with the responsive confidence of every class of the population in Germany and Prussia.

Not dazzled by the splendour of great achievements, I shall be content, if hereafter it be said of my government, that it was beneficial to my people, useful to my country, and a blessing to the Empire!

Your affectionate,

FREDERICK, I.R.

Berlin, March 12, 1888.

Henderson, Rait, & Spalding, Printers, Marylebone Lane, London, W.

www.ingramcontent.com/pod-product-compliance
Lightning Source LLC
Chambersburg PA
CBHW030536040726
47497CB00008B/2479